"You're Up For More?" Shannon Said With A Laugh.

"Now that's a loaded question," Ian replied.

Her expression quickly changed from confusion to embarrassed surprise. "You're incredible," she muttered.

"That's what I've been trying to tell you." He cupped his hand over her thigh to keep her from vaulting out of the chair.

Shannon removed his hand and rose. Ian watched her swift retreat in amusement. He was getting to her. No more than she had gotten to him. He needed to alleviate this fevered preoccupation with her, and he knew only two ways to accomplish that. He could give up and return to his solitary way of life. Or he could put aside his inherent distrust and open his mind to the possibility of a long-term relationship.

Just the thought caused his stomach muscles to contract painfully. There had to be a middle ground between the two.

Dear Reader,

This month Silhouette Desire brings you six brand-new, emotional and sensual novels by some of the bestselling— and most beloved—authors in the romance genre. Cait London continues her hugely popular miniseries THE TALLCHIEFS with *The Seduction of Fiona Tallchief,* April's MAN OF THE MONTH. Next, Elizabeth Bevarly concludes her BLAME IT ON BOB series with *The Virgin and the Vagabond.* And when a socialite confesses her virginity to a cowboy, she just might be *Taken by a Texan,* in Lass Small's THE KEEPERS OF TEXAS miniseries.

Plus, we have Maureen Child's *Maternity Bride, The Cowboy and the Calendar Girl,* the last in the OPPOSITES ATTRACT series by Nancy Martin, and Kathryn Taylor's tale of domesticating an office-bound hunk in *Taming the Tycoon.*

I hope you enjoy all six of Silhouette Desire's selections this month—and every month!

Regards,

Melissa Senate

Senior Editor
Silhouette Books

Please address questions and book requests to:
Silhouette Reader Service
U.S.: 3010 Walden Ave., P.O. Box 1325, Buffalo, NY 14269
Canadian: P.O. Box 609, Fort Erie, Ont. L2A 5X3

KATHRYN
TAYLOR
TAMING THE TYCOON

SILHOUETTE *Desire*®
Published by Silhouette Books
America's Publisher of Contemporary Romance

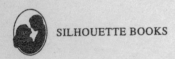

SILHOUETTE BOOKS

ISBN 0-373-76140-6

TAMING THE TYCOON

Printed in U.S.A.

KATHRYN TAYLOR's

passion for romance novels began in her late teens and left her with an itch to discover the world. After living in places as culturally diverse as Athens, Greece, and Cairo, Egypt (where she met and married her own romantic hero), she returned to the States, and she and her husband settled in the quiet village of Warwick, New York. Kathryn says, "Although my writing allows my mind to soar in the clouds, I have an energetic ten-year-old who keeps my feet planted on the ground."

To Fouad and Jasmin,
for accepting if not understanding
my obsession with writing.
A special thanks to my family for their support
and my critique partners for keeping me on track.

One

"What do you mean, I have a sister?" Ian Bradford came to his feet and leveled a stony glare at the middle-aged attorney seated behind the mahogany desk. "There has to be a mistake."

Richard Jenkins had been the family lawyer for more years than Ian could remember. His dealings with the man had been more cordial and more frequent than his dealings with his father.

"There's no mistake, Ian. Here's a copy of the birth certificate."

He grabbed the official document with the raised seal. His father's heart attack hadn't been as big of a shock as this latest revelation. "Two years old?"

"Nearly three," Jenkins mumbled.

"What the hell's the difference? He was well into his sixties."

Jenkins puffed up indignantly. "You don't give up sex after forty."

Ian let out a bitter laugh. "My old man sure didn't."

Wesley Bradford had been in the throes of a mid-life crisis for the past thirty years, but he had always prided himself on the fact that, after his divorce, no other woman had been able to land him.

"It says here that the mother was only twenty-five. Tiffany Moore. What kind of name is that? It sounds like a lamp." Ian grunted in disgust. "Twenty-five? Well, he did like them young."

"Your father had a lot of charisma."

"My father had a lot of money. That was the extent of his charm. Take it from someone who knew him better than most."

Ian glanced at the document again. If his father had been so proud of his daughter, why had he not allowed her to bear his name? A woman could claim any man as the father on a birth certificate. Especially when a share in a successful company was involved. This unknown child and her scheming mother deserved no part of that company.

"We'll see about this," Ian snarled. "You better believe I'll demand a blood test."

Jenkins shook his head. "Don't you think Wesley insisted on that before he agreed to pay child support? The results are in the file."

"And the child's mother? Where is she living now?"

"She died six months ago in a car accident. Your

sister lives with her aunt in some small town in upstate New York.''

''I don't have a sister.''

''Call her what you want. Chelsea Moore is Wesley's daughter, and according to the terms of the will she owns half of Westervelt Properties.''

Ian groaned. His father had picked a cruel way to acknowledge his paternal obligations to both his offspring. Why didn't he leave his bastard his money? Ian neither wanted nor needed that. He was glad now that his grandfather hadn't come with him today. The bequests would only rub salt in an old wound. No doubt, Wesley couldn't resist one more twist of the knife, even from the grave.

Ian had waited twenty years to fulfill the promise he had made when he was little more than a child. No one would take this from him now. No one.

''If I contest the will?''

''You don't have grounds.'' Jenkins furrowed his eyebrows in consternation, then broke out in a sly grin. ''You could sue for the administrative rights of your sister's inheritance. A judge might look more favorably on a sibling bond than that of an unmarried aunt. Especially when you're more familiar with the company.''

''Do it.''

''Whoa, Ian. That's not my field. I'll have to work with someone on this one.''

''Fine. Have your secretary draw up the necessary papers for me to sign today.'' Ian leaned back, allowing himself to relax for the first time since reading his father's will. "What do you know about this *aunt?*"

"She'll be here in a half an hour. You can judge for yourself. I wanted to meet with you first because I know your feelings about your father's company."

"My grandfather's company," Ian corrected.

"Wesley bought—"

Ian's fist came down on the table. "He swindled it."

Absently, Jenkins fidgeted with his tie. He could defend his client until hell froze over, but both he and Ian knew the truth.

While Ian's mother recuperated from cancer surgery in a hospital, Wesley had used the power of attorney rights she'd granted him to transfer her shares of Westervelt Properties to himself. Adding them to his own shares, he controlled fifty-one percent of the company, which he'd used to force Ian's grandfather out as president.

Jenkins drummed his fingers on the desktop. "Why don't you meet with the woman and see if you can come to some sort of terms before beginning a legal battle that could drag on for a couple of years?"

"What good would that do?"

"The way it stands now, the child's shares are to be held in a trust to be administered by her guardian. Maybe she'll find it a lesser risk to sell the shares and hold the trust in cash."

"Let's hope you're right."

The lawyer shook his head sorrowfully. "Then

control that Bradford temper of yours. I know that Wesley never treated you or your mother fairly…''

He waved his hand to cut Jenkins off. Ian wouldn't accept sympathy from a man who had helped his father cheat his grandparents out of their family business. "Spare me the sermon. Give me what you've got on the aunt. I like to know what I'm up against before I go into a meeting."

Ian thumbed through the folder of his father's personal papers. The compilation of material Wesley had gathered about his former mistress and her mother was a testament to his devious and distrustful nature. Not that he'd been completely wrong. Both women had attached themselves to wealthy older men. Unfortunately for Ian, his father apparently had seen no need to have the sister investigated, as well.

Shannon Moore checked the address on the envelope. Richard Jenkins, Esquire. Suite 218. She wasn't sure why she had come. Certainly the lawyer could have forwarded a copy of the will. After all, Wesley Bradford had never acknowledged his daughter while he was alive. And he had been more than willing to terminate child support payments after Tiffany's untimely death. Although the decision to refuse the money had been Shannon's, if the man had cared a wit, he would have put up a fight for his child.

After smoothing her linen skirt over her hips, she opened the outer door and stepped inside the plush offices.

A receptionist glanced up from her desk. "Miss Moore?"

"Yes."

"Mr. Jenkins is expecting you." She lifted the phone and announced Shannon's arrival. "First door on the right."

Shannon nodded and walked down the corridor. A man met her in the hall and extended his hand. "Thank you for coming, Miss Moore. I'm Richard Jenkins."

She smiled and allowed him to guide her into the conference room.

Inside, a second man rose from his seat at the table and nodded in her direction. "Miss Moore."

His silk suit and gold watch spoke of wealth, but the calloused hand he offered told of a man who had earned his money with hard work. He eased back into the leather chair and raised his lips in an arrogant grin. Ice blue eyes appraised her, unsettling her in a way she hadn't felt in years. Blatantly sexual with a hint of danger, he was everything she avoided in a man.

"This is Ian Bradford," Jenkins said, sounding as uncomfortable as she felt.

So, he was Wesley Bradford's son. In appearance, the two looked nothing alike, but she would guess he had inherited his father's ruthless streak. If she had known she was walking into an ambush, she would have come prepared.

She tipped her head in his direction. "Mr. Bradford. I'm sorry about your father."

He answered with a curt nod and a stone-cold glare.

Mr. Jenkins pointed to a chair. "Have a seat and we can get started."

She slid into the chair. "Should I have brought my attorney with me?"

Ian leaned forward and rested his elbows on the table. Well-defined muscles tested the stitching of his designer suit. "Is there a reason you think you need one?"

Shannon met his unwavering gaze and refused to back down. She was long past the days of allowing herself to be intimidated by any man. If her thirty-two years of life had taught her anything, it was that most men knew how to exploit weakness to their advantage. "I'm not sure yet. You two arranged this little meeting. Why don't you tell me?"

"I assure you there is nothing out of order going on here," Jenkins interjected, as if trying to ease the tension.

Ian raked a hand though his silky brown hair. "I do believe Ms. Moore is suspicious of us. Why is that?"

"Let's just say I'm reserving judgment until I hear what you have to say."

Jenkins pushed a large folder across the table. "I have highlighted the portion of the will that pertains to your ward, Chelsea Moore. If you'll just skip to page six…"

"Oh, let her read all of it, Richard. We wouldn't want her to miss any of the illustrious Bradford secrets."

Shannon slipped on her glasses and began reading the rather lengthy document. She noted that Ian was not given a copy so she had to assume he had already read the will. She skimmed over the instructions for the funeral arrangements and picked up with the bequests. By page two, she understood why the will made Mr. Jenkins uneasy and Ian Bradford downright bitter.

Wesley Bradford had left every one of his former mistresses a cash endowment. Including her sister and the two even younger ladies that he had carried on with afterward, the count was eighteen women. Her assessment of the man from their one and only meeting had been correct. He had been a cold, unfeeling bastard.

Shannon raised her eyes to glance at Ian's cynical smirk. Like father, like son. She shivered. "I think I'll just take this home and read it later."

"You're here now. I'd prefer you stay. There is something I'd like to discuss with you." Ian leaned forward in the chair, completely blocking her view of the attorney.

Jenkins rose and pulled nervously at the cuffs of his jacket. "I'll go get us some coffee."

Shannon nodded and scanned her eyes over the highlighted paragraph. She tried to keep her face expressionless as she read the part about Chelsea's fifty percent interest in Westervelt Properties. Her niece probably wouldn't have to worry about her college education. Unless the inheritance was what Ian Bradford wanted to discuss.

"I assume you plan to contest the will," she said dryly.

"I can't, as Mr. Jenkins will undoubtedly confirm when he returns. However, I'd be interested in purchasing the shares belonging to your ward."

"My niece," she countered angrily. "Who also happens to be your sister."

"I don't have a sister. My father, unfortunately, had a daughter," he muttered through clenched teeth.

Shannon thought of the solemn child who had come to live with her six months ago. Poor Chelsea didn't have much of a family to look up to. Her mother had used her as a meal ticket. She would never know her father. Even Shannon, who did her best to provide a loving environment, had to admit she lacked maternal instincts. Add to that menagerie a brother who refused to acknowledge her and Chelsea didn't have the makings of a happy life ahead.

Ian watched her, the rigid set of his jaw and his narrowed eyes barely concealing his irritation. He twisted his hands together in a gesture of impatience. "Well?"

"You want me to give you an answer right now?"

"You won't get a better offer."

"I'm not even sure what the company entails. You expect me to make a decision on Chelsea's behalf, with absolutely no information and only your altruistic and unbiased promise that I'm being offered a fair deal? Do I appear to be stupid, Mr. Bradford?"

"Not at all, Ms. Moore. I'm sure you're very smart." His compliment sounded more like an accusation.

"Then don't play me for a fool."

"I was merely presenting you with the opportunity to hold the child's inheritance in cash. After all, a lot of things can happen before she turns eighteen. Profitable companies have been known to fold for no apparent reason."

Was he threatening her or only trying to frighten her into making an immediate decision? "How old are you, Mr. Bradford?"

His eyebrows furrowed in confusion. "Thirty-three. What does that have to do with anything?"

"You're a little old to be playing If-I-can't-have-it-all-no-one-can." She collected the papers from the desk. "If you'll excuse me, I have nothing more to say to you."

Ian came to his feet at the same time as Shannon. "Well, I do."

"Speak through your lawyer in the future. Your communication skills are lacking."

"Meaning?"

"First of all, if you think you can scare me with your intimidation tactics, you've miscalculated."

"And?" His insolent half grin sent a heated jolt of resentment surging through her. She fought a losing battle to maintain self-control.

"When you want something from someone, it's

advantageous to try being nice instead of insulting your victim.''

''Is that something you learned while growing up in the slums?''

Shannon drew in a deep breath. Obviously, he'd had her background investigated. Did he think that because her family had spent a couple of years financially strapped while her mother went back to school, she would jump at any offer of money? The inheritance didn't even belong to her.

''This is getting us nowhere. Let me know when you've got something worthwhile to say.'' She tucked the manila folder under her arm and left the office.

Ian watched her retreat with more interest than was healthy in his present situation. Her long, shapely legs and slim hips moved in a graceful stride despite her evident ire. Once she disappeared from sight, he lowered himself into the chair again. Reining in his disappointment was easier than bringing his hormone level back to normal.

Shannon Moore was one interesting contradiction. A controlled business facade hid the street fighter beneath. Her auburn, collar-length hair framed an oval face and a fringe of bangs drew attention to a pair of huge brown eyes that turned golden with anger.

''What did you say to her, Ian?'' Jenkins asked as he came into the conference room. ''She stormed out of here at gale force.''

''I made her an offer. She wanted some time to think it over.'' No doubt she was on the way to her attorney's office right this moment. He shrugged. She was only a guardian of the trust. Once she learned that she had no say in the running of the company, his offer would start to look good to her.

"She's nothing like her sister, I can say that for her."

"I wouldn't know."

Jenkins grinned. "Sure you would. Tiffany Moore. She was the one who showed up at your second cousin's wedding in the leopard bodysuit. Remember?"

Ian recalled the flashy, brassy blonde with the piercing laughter who had made several passes at him. To say his father's date elicited more stares than the pregnant bride in the white wedding dress was an understatement. "You have to be joking. She was Shannon's sister?"

While his father's investigation into his mistress's background had turned up Shannon's childhood, as well, Ian had no idea how Shannon supported herself now. By her cool, articulate manner, he would guess she had risen above her humble beginnings. She had acquired the social skills and polish her younger sister lacked.

"We have a few things to discuss, Ian."

He returned his attention to his father's lawyer. "Get things started. If she hasn't gotten back to you in a month, file the petition with the courts."

"All right. Now, on to a different matter. Wesley paid child support to the mother. Am I to assume with both parties deceased, the arrangement is now terminated?"

Ian gave the question serious thought. He saw no purpose in antagonizing the woman until he knew precisely what she wanted. "No. Send the money to Shannon until she makes up her mind about the company."

Jenkins cocked one eyebrow. *"Shannon?"*

"Miss Moore."

"Be careful, Ian, or you might find yourself falling victim to the same weakness you despised in your father."

Ian's lips curved up in a sardonic smile. "There are two big differences. I'm not married and I stick to women born in the same decade as me."

He closed the file and exhaled a groan. He would not allow the minor development of his attraction to Shannon steer him from his course of action. Westervelt Properties *would* be returned to his grandfather, no matter what he had to do to fulfill that promise.

Shannon tossed the folder and her keys on the hall table. The one-hour train ride from New York City had given her time to regroup before trying to deal with an energetic child. After checking her mail, she walked across the small front lawn to the house next door. A row of red tulips in the window box signaled the true arrival of spring. The aroma of baking bread lingered as she stepped into the kitchen.

"Oh, Betty Crocker. Where are you?"

"Just a sec." A moment later Wendy Sommers strolled into the room. A mop of brown curls bounced to the spring in her step. "How was the meeting?"

Shannon rolled her shoulders to relieve the tension at the base of her neck. "More interesting than I had expected."

Her friend held up a cup. "Coffee?"

"Please." She dropped into a chair and rested her arms on the glass tabletop. "Chelsea's brother was there."

"And?" Wendy prodded.

"When I met Wesley Bradford, I thought no one could be more overbearing. Apparently arrogance is a dominant gene. He passed it on to Ian."

"*Ian* seems to have made quite an impression on you."

Shannon grimaced at Wendy's inquisitive tone. He'd made an impression, all right. One she didn't want to admit to, even to herself. "How was Chelsea?"

"She was great. But she missed her auntie Shane."

"Did she?" she asked a bit uncertainly.

When Shannon had found herself the guardian of a toddler, she panicked. What she knew about children would fit on the head of a pin. To give Chelsea some semblance of a normal life she had returned to the small suburban town where she had spent her teenage years, armed with a library of parenting books.

Finding a high school classmate as her neighbor had eased her return. Wendy's outgoing nature and blind acceptance of others' imperfections gave Shannon her first real friend.

"What's my little princess up to?" Shannon asked.

"She's watching 'Sesame Street' with Anna." Wendy placed a tray on the table and took a seat. "So tell me more about Mr. Bradford. If he's Chelsea's brother, does that make you his aunt?"

"Very funny. Actually, I was a little disappointed. I thought…well, never mind what I thought." Taking a deep breath, Shannon pushed the troubling concerns from her mind. "He's made it clear he plans to uphold that Bradford family tradition of ignoring Chelsea's existence."

Wendy stared thoughtfully, then let out a small giggle. "Why, Shannon Moore, you're nothing more than a closet optimist. You figured he would learn about his sister and he'd be bursting with sibling love and pride."

Hearing her delusional fantasies described like that, Shannon realized how naive she was. She took a sip of coffee and leaned back in the chair with a wistful sigh. "Maybe I did. But if you tell anyone, I'll deny it. I have a reputation to maintain in this town as a high-powered, no-nonsense barracuda."

"But a barracuda who shows us how to invest our money. And we love you for it. Not to mention that you keep a lot of us employed."

"Because I can't do anything pertaining to house maintenance by myself." Shannon blessed the education and the business connections that allowed her to continue serving her clients and still be at home for Chelsea. Otherwise the upkeep on a house would have been beyond her means. "And this mothering thing is a whole lot tougher than Donna Reed and June Cleaver made it out to be."

"Suzy Homemaker, you ain't," Wendy agreed. "Give up those ridiculous books on raising children and follow your instincts. As long as love is there, you'll do fine."

Shannon sighed. Where her friend's house smelled of potpourri and fresh-baked pies, she usually had to air out the odor of burned cookies. As for following her instincts, she had none. Her own parents' self-serving emotional tugs-of-war had left her unprepared for the role of a supportive parent.

"I'm glad I wasn't looking for a sympathetic shoulder." She could only hope her friend was right and her love for the little girl who had taken up residence in her heart would be enough.

"Do you want me to lie to you?" Wendy asked.

"Please. I've had about as much of the truth as I can stand today."

"Lord, Shannon. I've never known you to let any man rattle you. Even when we were back in high school."

"I'm not rattled. I'm in complete control."

If that were true, why had Ian been able to provoke her into losing her temper, something no man had ever done before? How had his stone-cold glare generated an unfamiliar heat in her? She couldn't be attracted to the man.

Then why couldn't she banish his image from her mind?

Two

Ian glanced around the office. The old cherrywood furniture he'd dragged up from storage returned the room to the way he remembered it from his childhood visits. No matter how much of the past he tried to recreate, one fact could not be denied. His grandfather was not yet the sole owner of Westervelt Properties again.

In the past few weeks Ian had prepared himself for an inevitable showdown with Shannon Moore. Actually, he had been looking forward to another meeting. Why hadn't she contacted him or Jenkins? He didn't believe she would walk away from the inheritance without a fight. At the very least, he figured she would take the money. The only thing he hadn't expected was her silence.

After twenty years, a two-week wait should be

easy. It had been hell. What was her game? Instead of turning over the daily running of the company to his grandfather as he had planned, he had come in every day expecting to hear from her. He had to get back to his own business.

He scanned the mail then tossed it aside. His gaze returned to the pile. The top letter had no return address, but the Walton, New York, postmark struck a familiar chord. He slit open the top of the envelope and removed the contents. Between a folded slip of paper were two halves of a child support check written out to Shannon Moore.

Shannon sucked in a deep, calming breath. Her cream-colored slacks had a bright red stain on the leg and a pile of SpaghettiOs covered one suede pump. The plastic bowl Chelsea had tossed from the table rolled around the kitchen floor. Only yesterday the pasta dish had been the child's favorite.

"That wasn't nice, Chelsea. Say 'I'm sorry.'" Shannon kept her voice quiet but stern.

"No."

"You have to apologize or go to your room for a time-out."

Chelsea folded her small arms across her chest and pushed out her chin. "No."

Shannon tried to recall what the book said to do in this situation. *Lose your temper and you lose control.* Had Dr. What's-his-name ever worn a bowl of spaghetti? *Limit your admonitions to the deed, not the child.*

She placed her hand on Chelsea's shoulder. "I'm very disappointed by your behavior."

An earth-curdling scream reverberated around the room. Shannon's jaw dropped. How could such a horrific sound come from a little girl? She reached for the book on the counter and thumbed though the chapter on temper tantrums.

What was she doing wrong? Her every attempt to reach the petulant child had failed. Chelsea shied away from demonstrative gestures and met friendly overtures with wary silence.

Chelsea's psychologist had assured Shannon that Chelsea would emerge from her introverted shell when she got used to her new surroundings. Was this show of defiance an improvement? During her years as a Wall Street broker Shannon had handled nervous and often angry clients with detached calm, yet one small child reduced her to near helplessness.

She tossed the book in the garbage and fell back on the same strategy she used when dealing with any irrational adult. She walked away for a cooling-off period. A headache pounded against her temples. To make matters worse, the doorbell rang. She had visions of the police breaking down the front door and arresting her on child endangerment charges.

Obviously, parenthood had taken what little sanity she had once possessed.

Just when she thought she had hit bottom, she opened the door to find Ian Bradford leaning against the support beam on her front porch. His deep blue eyes ran an appraising gaze over her un-flattering appearance. His laughter topped off an already rotten morning. She glanced over her shoulder at the child, then back to him.

"Is this a family visit?" she asked.

"Are you having a bad day?" Did he have to look so damned pleased?

"No. I normally walk around the house covered in tomato sauce while Chelsea serenades me in the key of C." Why didn't those child-rearing experts with their psychobabble warn her to change out of her business clothes before feeding a child? "What do you want?"

"May I come in?"

She waved her hand with a flourish. "Be my guest."

If nothing else, his arrival put an end to Chelsea's vocal tantrum. Within seconds, Shannon had a pint-size appendage attached to her leg, hindering her as she tried to show Ian into the living room.

"Have a seat. I have to get changed." Scooping the child up in her arms, she darted to her bedroom.

She plopped Chelsea on the bed and quickly shed her soiled slacks in favor of a brightly colored peasant skirt. Paired with her ruffled blouse, she looked like a Gypsy. She searched her closet for a better choice, then gave up. Why did she care? It wasn't as if she wanted to impress the man.

"Who he is?" Chelsea asked.

Shannon ran a brush though Chelsea's baby-fine hair and for the first time the child didn't flinch away. "He's your brother, Ian."

"Chelsea wants a cookie." Obviously, the discovery of a big brother was less appealing than Mrs. Fields's chocolate chip cookies.

"Not now." Braced for the worst, Shannon was pleasantly surprised when the child shrugged and turned her attention to the crystal perfume bottles on her vanity.

"I sorry," Chelsea said to the reflection in the mirror.

A little late, but Shannon got her apology. The simple words felt like a major triumph. "I know. Leave that for now. We have a guest."

They returned to the living room where Ian had made himself right at home in the overstuffed chair. Shannon noted the way he carefully avoided looking at his sister. Any hope that some sense of family obligation or even natural curiosity had compelled his visit faded in a flash. Her niece would continue to live without a male influence in her life.

"I expected to hear from you," Ian said.

"Did I say I would call?" She pushed a teddy bear out of the way and sat on the sofa. Chelsea scrambled into Shannon's lap and cuddled close.

"You returned my check."

"I didn't know what it was for."

"Child support for…ah…"

"Your sister?"

He exhaled slowly. "She's not my sister."

Shannon tenderly stroked the child's back, lulling her into a quiet, dreamlike state. "If you don't consider her family, then there's no reason for you to support her."

"I didn't mean it like that."

"Yes, you did."

Ian noted the quiet sorrow in her words. She seemed tired. Obviously the girl was a handful. Although right now, falling asleep in her aunt's lap, she looked like a little angel. He dragged his gaze away. He had no business feeling anything for this blue-eyed imp.

"Just tell me what you want," he said.

"Did I ask you for anything, Mr. Bradford?"

"No. As a matter of fact, you've been conspicuous by your silence. You must have a price. A bottom line?"

"You seem to be under the mistaken impression that I have something to sell. The inheritance belongs to Chelsea, not me."

"And as her legal guardian you make all decisions regarding her money and property until her eighteenth birthday."

She tucked a strand of hair behind her ear. "If those decisions are in *her* best interest, not yours."

"The money would allow you to afford some help with the child."

Her golden eyes flashed with anger. "Would you stop calling her 'the child'? Her name is Chelsea."

"Fine, Chelsea could have a nanny, you could hire a housekeeper…"

"So, now my house is dirty?" Her whispered words reflected her irritation as clearly as if she had shouted.

He glanced around the room at the assortment of toys that littered the obviously expensive furniture.

However, despite the presence of a two-year-old, the pale blue print sofa and chair were surprisingly spotless. "Not dirty, exactly."

"Perhaps you'd like to take a moment to get your foot out of your mouth."

Ian rose and paced around the room. Shannon had been right. His communication skills *were* lacking, but only around her. Normally, he made his point without leaving room for argument.

She carefully slipped out from underneath the child and lovingly tucked a small crocheted blanket around her tiny body. "She doesn't need nannies, cooks and housekeepers coming in and out of her life." Shannon stormed into the kitchen.

Ian followed. "Then why don't you tell me what the chi...Chelsea needs."

As she spun to face him, her full skirt swirled around her legs. "Time, Ian. She needs time and compassion and love from what little family she has left. Are you offering her your time in return for her shares in the company?"

"I beg your pardon?"

"It's not difficult to understand. You can deal with her now or when she's an eighteen-year-old stranger you didn't have the time or interest to know."

"I don't follow."

"You want your precious company. Fine." She leaned against the tile counter and folded her arms over her waist. Her full red lips curved upward in a challenging smile. "For the next twelve months you maintain a regular relationship with *your sister.*

At the end of the year you can buy her shares in the company.''

His eyes narrowed suspiciously. ''What's the catch?''

''No catch.''

''And if I refuse?''

She shook her head. ''I'm not about to make a bunch of empty threats. That's something you'll have to fight out with Chelsea fifteen years from now. The only decision you have to make is how long you want to wait for Westervelt Properties.''

''And you believe that blackmailing me into visiting my sister is in her best interest.''

Shannon met his gaze without blinking. Despite the fact that he towered a full head above her, she didn't show any sign of being intimidated. ''First of all, I'm not blackmailing you, I'm bribing you. And secondly, the idea must have some merit, since that's the first time you've referred to her as your sister.''

Ian bit back an angry retort. He still had the option of suing for control of Chelsea's inheritance, but he had no guarantee he'd win. He didn't like having his back against a wall. Shannon obviously knew how to manipulate a man. She might present a better package, but was she really any different than her gold-digging sister?

''What's in it for you?''

''Nothing.''

''Given your family history, I find that hard to believe.''

She arched her eyebrows. "And which history is that?"

"Your sister managed to get herself a substantial child support settlement. You mother married her wealthy patient less than a month after she began working as his private nurse."

"You had my mother investigated, too?" She blinked and he noted an unmistakable sadness in her shimmering eyes. "Don't you have anything better to do with your time and money?"

"I never had any of you investigated. That was Wesley's doing," he said, too defensively for his own liking. Where had this feeling of guilt come from? He'd never felt compelled to explain his actions to anyone.

"Oh, your father. That paragon of family values who was seduced and outwitted by his twenty-five-year-old manicurist."

"I never said he was blameless."

"They're both to blame but Chelsea is the only one who's left to pay." She pushed off the counter and walked to the Dutch door. "Why don't you go back to the city and try to figure out what's *in it for me*. I have a dirty house to clean right now." She gestured toward the alcove where the pile of spaghetti stained the white tile floor.

"Listen, Shannon…"

She opened the screen door. "Just go. We've both said enough for today. It will only get nastier."

She was throwing him out! He couldn't believe it.

Perhaps he should leave. He needed distance. Something inside him responded to her. Not in the obvious way, although in different circumstances, he probably would have been drawn to her cool, reserved beauty. She reached him on a different, more primitive level, bringing out the worst side of his nature. The part of him that reacted without thinking. She had the ability to disarm him and that made her a dangerous woman.

If her sister had possessed one-tenth of Shannon's allure, he could understand how his father had lost his head. And, God help him, if he wasn't careful, he could end up a casualty of the same fate.

Shannon watched from the front yard as Ian got in his sports car and drove away. When she turned to go back in the house, she saw Wendy sitting on her front stoop with a mischievous grin on her face.

"Now, that was a man!"

"You could have fooled me," Shannon grumbled.

"Put on your glasses, girl. He's gorgeous."

"He's also Chelsea's brother."

Wendy crossed the lawn and met her at the picket fence. "So that's the mysterious Ian. No wonder you haven't wanted to talk about him. You're keeping him all to yourself."

"You're a happily married mother of three."

"That doesn't mean I'm dead."

Shannon let out a puff of air. "That man isn't interested in any kind of long-term relationships."

"Who cares? That's the kind of man you have fun with. You don't have to marry him."

"I don't *have fun* with men."

"That's because you don't have one like him." Wendy sent her a sly wink. "If you're not interested, send him over here. I'll play house with him."

Shannon pressed her hand to her chest and feigned shock. "You're destroying my illusions of the demure suburban housewife."

"I know. You thought we sat around all day watching soap operas and swapping cake recipes while you career women got to eat power lunches and live out all your carnal fantasies."

"I never thought that you sat around all day and I certainly never lived out any of my carnal fantasies."

Her last relationship had ended due to lack of interest. The Saturday night dinners and the obligatory Tuesday night sex had been so routine as to be boring. With hindsight, she realized that all her liaisons had been with safe, dull, predictable men. Rather than chance a passionate romance that ended in a bitter feud like her parents', she chose to take no risks at all.

Somehow, she didn't imagine Ian would be predictable. Intense, exciting, maybe even dangerous, but never predictable.

She couldn't believe she was wondering about his male prowess. He didn't have one desirable quality to attract her in the first place. Except maybe, a body to die for. An involuntary smile tugged at the corner of her mouth and a shiver danced along her spine. This train of thought would land her in the kind of trouble she had successfully avoided up until now. She shook her head and focused on her friend's knowing smirk.

"Are you telling me that you're not the least bit interested?" Wendy asked.

"In a relationship with Ian?"

"No. In some pure, unadulterated knock-your-socks-off sex with him."

The hot flush crept up Shannon's cheeks. "Is nothing sacred to you?"

"I guess that means you are. Good. You need some fun in your life."

Shannon changed the subject. "Can you watch Chelsea tomorrow? I have to meet with a client in the city."

"No problem." Wendy bent down to pluck a weed from her flower bed. When she rose again, she handed Shannon a yellow daisy and asked innocently, "Doesn't Ian live in the city? If you decide you want to spend the night, I'll keep Chelsea..."

"Wendy. Stay out of my love life."

"You have to have one before I can stay out of it."

Muffling a yelp of frustration, Shannon stomped back to her house. Wendy meant well with her friendly probing, but Shannon wasn't used to discussing her private life. Although she had loved Tiffany dearly, they hadn't been the kind of sisters who traded confidences. They had both lived through the same trying and painful experiences but their lives had taken very different roads.

Shannon had put all her energies into a career so that she would never be dependent on the financial whims of a man. Before she'd received custody of Chelsea, the only commitment in her life had been a car loan.

Her sister, conversely, had begun a quest for a man who would keep her in style. If that man already had a wife, so much the better. When Tiffany began her affair with Wesley, she figured she had hit the mother lode. And for a while she lived very well, but as Wesley's interest started to wane, she had made sure she had a stranglehold on his wallet in the form of Chelsea.

Perhaps Ian had a right to feel bitter and angry. It must have been a shock to learn he had a sister young enough to be his daughter. Would he eventually get beyond his misgivings and open his heart to Chelsea as family? Did he even understand the concept?

Ian drove his car up the winding driveway that led to his grandfather's home. The large Colonial house was the only place Ian felt remotely comfortable. He had spent most of his childhood summers with his grandparents, back in the days when Wakefield, Connecticut, was still considered the country rather than an extended suburb of New York City. Despite the changes, he still enjoyed his visits.

Adam Westervelt was on the front lawn tending

his prized roses. At seventy-five, his grandfather was more active and fit than many men half his age. Fate hadn't been kind to the older man. In his lifetime Adam had buried his wife and both his children.

"Come see this, Ian." As he stepped from the car, Adam waved him over. "The American Beauty rose. Soft, delicate and beautiful. A lot like a woman, eh?"

"Including the thorns," Ian observed pointedly.

"You're a cynic."

"I'm a realist."

"Living your life alone is not reality, boy. Sharing your life, now that's real."

Ian stifled a groan. He wasn't up for another lecture on the virtues of marriage. There wasn't much he would refuse his grandfather, but he had no inclinations toward finding himself a wife. "I'm not here to discuss me. When will you be ready to take over Westervelt Properties again?"

"I appreciate what you're trying to do..."

"All I'm doing is returning what is rightfully yours."

Adam tossed his gardening gloves to the ground. "The only reason I felt bitter about Wesley's betrayal was because I wanted the company for you. It's yours now. The circle has come full turn."

"I have my own work and, quite honestly, investments, insurance and the like don't interest me. The company bears your name, and you're going to run it again."

Adam placed his hand on Ian's shoulder. Despite

the old man's protests, his eyes contained the first spark of excitement Ian had seen in years.

"Is your sister in agreement with this arrangement?"

"What?" Ian choked. He had not mentioned the specifics of Wesley's will and had instructed the lawyer not to, either.

"Did you think I wouldn't hear? That kind of news has a way of making the rounds."

Ian drew a deep breath. With eighteen ex-mistresses all receiving cash endowments, he shouldn't be surprised that some of them were bound to talk. Especially when a couple of the women lived in this very town. "I should have told you."

"I'm not surprised he had an illegitimate child. Considering the way he carried on, I'm surprised there aren't more. So, have you met her?"

"Yes."

"And does she have any interest in running the company?" Adam asked.

"Maybe in twenty years or so."

"I don't follow."

"She's two years old," Ian muttered in distaste.

Adam frowned. "Now, that does surprise me."

"Don't look so worried. One way or another, I'll be buying out her shares."

"I'm only disappointed because I'd hoped she'd be more of a contemporary of yours. You need family. I'm not going to be around forever and you show no signs of settling down to have a family of your own."

"I don't need one." Nor did he want the emotional roller-coaster ride that went along with any long-term relationship. Some women used sex to get what they wanted, and some withheld sex to achieve their goal. But in the end they all wanted the same thing—a ring on their finger and unlimited access to a credit line.

"Then why are you building yourself that freight empire? Who are you going to leave it to? Even Wesley, for all his faults, passed his possessions on to his children."

Ian refrained from mentioning that his father's will had been the final insult to a lifetime of injury. He had received the bulk of the cash assets, which he couldn't have cared less about. Westervelt Properties, which he did want, went in equal shares, but he would be responsible for managing the company. If he were spiteful, he could run the company into the ground, but he would not destroy something that bore his grandfather's name and was a source of pride to Adam. Also, taking an inheritance from a child would make him no better than his father.

His mind wandered to little Chelsea Moore. If Wesley had left his money to the child and the company to Ian, would he have been so quick to dismiss the blood bond between them? Probably not. She was his sister and no amount of denial would change that fact.

He thought about Shannon. If she did turn out to be like her social-climbing mother and her schem-

ing sister, who would be there to look out for Chelsea's interests?

Like it or not, he had to assume a role in his
sister's upbringing and keep an eye on Shannon
Moore at the same time. When he remembered the
golden-eyed woman who'd had the unmitigated gall
to ask him to leave her house, he laughed. Did she
always give as good as she got?

Ian grinned. This new position he had appointed
for himself was beginning to appeal to him.

Three

Shannon made one more run through the house. Not a toy or an article of clothing was out of place. She checked her watch for the third time in as many minutes. Why was she working herself into a state over Ian's visit? His crack about hiring a housekeeper had bothered her more than she'd realized. Keeping up with Chelsea while juggling her clients had taken a toll. If a few dolls and crayons didn't get put back on a shelf, that didn't make her a bad guardian.

Two months ago Ian hadn't known about his sister. Two weeks ago he was still denying any relationship to her. *Now* he wanted to come over and discuss her upbringing? Who the hell did he think he was? For the past half year she had been raising

Chelsea without financial or emotional support from the Bradfords.

With Chelsea at preschool for the morning, Shannon figured she wouldn't have to mind her words when Ian invariably said something to tick her off. Why did she allow him to get to her?

She still had an hour left before he was due and, seeing a speck of lint on the gray carpet, she pulled the vacuum out again. Cranking up the volume on the CD player to be heard above the drone, she began her task. The sheer boredom of the chore made her look for ways to amuse herself while working.

The amplifiers blared with a classic disco song. Shannon bowed to her vacuum. "Would you care to dance?"

As a partner, Hoover was on the short side, but his powerful beater bar propelled him over the carpet with ease, if not grace. If she overlooked the fact that she had to lead, he did a mean hustle.

The music ended and she curtsied to her date. "Thank you, kind sir."

A round of applause broke the silence. Shannon let out a yelp and whirled around. Ian filled the archway between the foyer and living room, his aloof grin mocking her. Her heart beat double-time, more from fright than physical exertion.

"The door was open. Had I known you were already entertaining, I would have waited outside."

"You're early," she sputtered.

Once again Ian had caught her off balance with his brilliant sense of timing. Did he possess some kind of radar that allowed him to zero in on her at the worst possible moment?

"The traffic was light. I made good time."

"Couldn't you have stopped for coffee somewhere?"

"I didn't realize your busy schedule was so inflexible."

"Do you think I just sit around all day?"

He wasn't in the house for two minutes and already he had her on the defensive. His tailored suit screamed "Power," while her tattered jeans and tie-dyed shirt said "Woodstock groupie." More unsettling were the piercing blue eyes that appraised her with a scorching intensity.

After tucking the vacuum back into the closet, she gestured toward the sofa. "Have a seat."

"Where's Chelsea?"

"School."

He lowered himself into the plump cushion with lazy ease. "Isn't she young for that?"

Shannon shrugged. "Nursery school."

"Oh. What do you do while she's in school?"

"I keep busy."

"In this town?"

She planted both hands firmly on her hips. "What's wrong with this town?"

"Nothing. Are we going to start with an argument or can we save that for the finale when you kick me out again?"

Was she being overly sensitive? She had decided to move Chelsea to Walton precisely because it was a small town. The quiet and safety had been the biggest drawing points. Sucking in a calming breath, she dropped into the chair across from Ian. "What did you want to talk about?"

"The company. Your offer. Mostly Chelsea's future."

Her eyebrow arched in question. "Why the sudden change of attitude?"

"I don't know what you mean."

"Last time you were here I got the distinct impression you didn't think Chelsea deserved anything."

"I reacted inappropriately and I'm sorry." His apology seemed out of character. She searched his face for some sign of emotion, either sincere or faked, but his features remained impassive.

"Forget it."

"I brought you some information about the company." He removed a thick envelope from his pocket and handed it across the table.

As she reached out, his calloused fingers brushed over hers. The physical reaction was swift and acute, causing her to gasp. Hoping to deny the tingling sensations running rampant, she retracted her hand and muttered, "Static electricity."

"Right." Ian stifled a chuckle. Her cheeks had turned the same red shade as his grandfather's American Beauty. This was not the same woman he had met in Jenkins's office, or even the one he had seen a couple weeks ago. Shannon Moore had many different facets.

He had deliberately arrived early to catch her off guard and his plan had paid off. The rigid armor of control she wore to keep people at a distance seemed to have deserted her. Her startled response to their accidental contact had been no more shocking to her than to him.

He, too, felt the seductive connection between them. And he, too, felt the need to deny it. "Anyway. If there's anything there you don't understand, I'd be happy to explain it to you."

Shannon swiped her glasses off the coffee table and slipped them on. "I have no intention of interfering in the way you run the company."

"That's the problem. I don't plan to run Westervelt Properties. Investment strategy is not my specialty. I plan to turn over the running of the company to someone more qualified in the field."

"Did you have someone in mind?" A spark of interest ignited her amber eyes. Or was it distrust he saw reflected?

"It's already taken care of."

"Oh." He wasn't sure but he thought he heard a hint of disappointment in her voice. Had she expected him to consult with her first?

As she glanced through the pamphlets, he used the moment to study her. Sunlight filtering in from the bay window cast a fiery glow over her hair. Faded denim jeans molded the long legs she had tucked beneath her nicely rounded bottom. He recalled her uninhibited dance number and the uncomfortable reaction he'd experienced from the sight. That same tension returned. Who was he kidding? His present condition had little to do with tension and a lot to do with desire. He shifted in the seat and let out a muffled groan.

Shannon fixed her gaze on him. "Did you say something?"

What she did to his insides with just a look defied logic. His plan to catch her off balance and keep her there was backfiring in a big way. "Do you need anything explained?"

"No." She rolled her shoulders and rubbed her fingers over the back of her neck. The gesture, while seemingly innocent, was purely provocative. Her full breasts strained against the T-shirt.

He cleared his throat. "I need Chelsea's social security number. I can't seem to find it in my father's papers."

"Why?"

"For business reasons. She is a partner right now. And while I remember, you'll be receiving the monthly support checks again, so—"

"No," she said firmly.

"Why?"

"I will not be paid like some baby-sitter to care for my niece."

"My sister."

She sprang to her feet and tossed the papers onto the coffee table. "Then act like her brother, not some trustee appointed to care for her needs. You haven't spent ten minutes with her yet. You have no idea what she needs."

"If you don't mind my asking, how do you plan to support her?"

"I've done just fine without you up to this point,

Ian. I own the house and I pick up work on a free-lance basis.'' Her eyes blazed with indignation.

''Then I don't understand what you want from me.''

''I don't want anything from you. I thought we were discussing Chelsea.'' She slid her hands into her pockets and leaned against the mantel surrounding a stone fireplace.

''Don't you think the thirty-year age difference will make it difficult for us to become friends?''

''Friends will come and go out of her life. Family is forever and age has nothing to do with the relationship.''

His gaze traveled slowly over her rigid frame. This family issue seemed very important to her. Given what he knew of her background, he couldn't understand why. ''You realize, of course, that being a constant influence in her life would make me a constant presence in yours.''

''Every silver lining has a cloud,'' she said dryly.

''Your overwhelming enthusiasm is touching,'' he replied.

''Forgive my cynicism, but let's not pretend you're here for any other reason than to get Chelsea's share of the company. I'm making sure she gets something valuable out of the deal, as well.''

Although he deserved the anger, her low opinion of him cut deep. Unlike his father, he had no intention of cheating his sister out of anything she was entitled to. ''I'm not here only to get her share of the company.''

''Why else?''

"I'll be looking over your shoulder to make sure her money is handled properly."

Looking over her shoulder? More like breathing down her neck. Shannon groaned. "Money! Is that all you think about? Do you go to sleep at night and dream of dollar signs?"

A hint of amusement sparked in his eyes. "Do you really what to know what I dream about when I'm alone in bed?" he muttered in a sexy drawl.

"Let's just stick to the point."

"Hell, I've forgotten what the point is." His seductive smile disarmed her.

She tried to ignore the butterflies fluttering in her stomach. The man was as cold and distant as a polar ice cap yet her traitorous body reacted to him in a deliciously warming way. Why would she set herself up for a fall? Ian had made his feelings for her known from the beginning. He believed that, like her sister, she was out for the Bradford money.

When he had mentioned hiring a manager for Westervelt Properties she had foolishly imagined he'd been considering her. After all, investment strategy was her specialty. Apparently he didn't realize that, because he seemed to think she needed financial help from him just to run her house. If she pointed out her qualifications now, he would probably assume she was looking for a job and reiterate his offer of money.

She stood tall and tried to look confident despite her appearance. Clothes might not make the person, but in her case, they did help reinforce the image she hoped to project. Right now, she had the poise of a babbling high school teenager in the presence of a movie star. "The point is Chelsea. Can I assume that you'd like to set up some sort of schedule for visitation privileges?"

"By all means, do assume that."

He was patronizing her. Shannon wanted to tell him where to go. Instead she reminded herself that this arrangement would ultimately benefit Chelsea. In the last six months the child had become the center of her world. A major about-face for a woman who'd vowed never to allow emotions to rule her heart.

Only last week Chelsea had announced at preschool that she had a new brother. That took some explaining to the teacher. In her almost-three-year-old mind, having a brother made her more like the other children in her class. Chelsea needed family in her life even if dealing with Ian was the price Shannon had to pay.

"Why don't you tell me how you want to proceed," she suggested.

"Could we just let it happen?"

"What do you mean?"

"I'm a stranger to her. Do you think she will allow me to pick her up and take her places in the beginning?"

"So, maybe I haven't worked out a few of the details." She had been certain he would refuse the offer.

"I'd say not." He rose and crossed the room to stand next to her on the hearth. His masculine scent acted like electrodes, jolting her senses. "Especially how we're going to deal with this...tension between us."

She took a step back. "I'm sure the anger will defuse in time."

"That's not the kind of tension I was referring to. I was referring to the sexual awareness that neither one of us can ignore. I want you, and you want me, too."

She folded her arms across her chest, refusing to acknowledge the truth of his words. "Arrogant and conceited. What a charming combination. You also happen to be dead wrong."

"Am I?" He pulled off her glasses and placed them on the hearth. Cupping her chin between his thumb and forefinger, he tilted her head back. "Am I?"

She unconsciously moistened her lips. Her heart thumped against her ribs. "Yes."

"Yes?" He smiled and lowered his head until their faces were inches apart.

"No."

"Yes or no, Shannon?"

He had her so flustered she wasn't sure what question she was answering. Before she could stop him, he brushed his mouth over hers.

A ribbon of heat uncurled deep inside her. The brief kiss was stirring yet left her strangely unsatisfied. She touched a finger to her lips. The taste of him lingered, leaving her hungry for more. She couldn't suppress a sigh.

"I like the fringe benefits of this arrangement." Ian's whispered words caressed her ear.

Had she lost her mind? When she focused enough to see his smug grin, she knew the answer. What had been a profound and enlightening moment for her had been nothing more than a means to prove his point.

She turned her head to free herself from his hold. "That isn't part of the bargain."

"Too bad. Then you would get something out of the deal, as well."

Sure! Like a whole lot more trouble than he was worth. "You flatter yourself."

"You're the one who flatters me, Shannon. Your wistful sigh and racing pulse gave me quite an ego boost. Or are you still going to deny the spark of electricity there?"

She tipped her head back to gaze at his self-righteous expression. "I can stick my finger in a wall socket and get the same kind of shock with a lot less aggravation."

His rich laughter mocked her. "I thought you had more guts than to walk away from a challenge."

"I have more sense than to walk blindly into a minefield." An affair with Ian would be a dangerous proposition. Between Chelsea and her clients, Shannon just didn't have enough stamina left to play games with so formidable an opponent as Ian.

The blare of a car horn cut off Ian's reply. Shannon muttered a thanks to the heavens and went to the front door. Her hasty and relieved retreat could mean only one thing. She was more interested than she wanted to be.

He smiled. She would take a bit of coaxing, but

then he never had enjoyed anything that came too easily. He didn't feel the slightest twinge of guilt about pursuing her. Despite her protestations to the contrary, she was interested, too. Neither of them were kids anymore. They knew exactly what they were getting into. He couldn't think of one good reason why they shouldn't let the passion between them run its course.

And then, one good reason came bouncing into the room, rambling on nonstop with her aunt. A kinetic ball of energy with a pair of bright blue eyes, little Chelsea reminded him of the reason he was here. Not to get involved with Shannon but to keep an eye on her.

"Say hello to your brother," Shannon said. "He came to see you today." Her smile masked the challenging edge in her words.

Chelsea's childish chatter ended the second she saw him. She hid behind her aunt's leg and buried her face against the worn denim jeans. A sheet of paper was clutched firmly in her hand.

"Are you going to say hi?" Shannon asked. Her fingers smoothed the child's blond curls. When she didn't get a response, she turned toward Ian and shrugged. "Maybe if you sat you wouldn't seem so big to her."

He crouched in front of Chelsea. "You're not afraid of me, are you? You're a big girl, right?"

She raised her head and fixed a curious gaze on him. Lips pursed together, she nodded her shy agreement.

"And an artist, too." He eased the paper from

her small hand. Afraid to offend the child by mis-
interpreting the jumble of colored lines, he smiled
and said, "I can't see well without my glasses.
What is this a picture of?"

"Aunt Shane, Chelsea and puppy."

"You have a puppy?" he asked. She shook her
head. "Do you want one?"

Her face lit up with expectation.

Shannon glared murderously at him, then offered
a smile toward the girl. "You have to eat lunch
now, Chels."

"Sketti?" Chelsea asked hopefully.

Shannon hadn't served that particular dish since
the unpleasant feeding incident the last time Ian had
been there. She ruffled the child's hair. "Okay. But
you have to change out of your school clothes
first."

Chelsea scooted around him and skipped down
the hall to her room.

When Ian rose, he noted that Shannon's warm
smile had disappeared. "Don't do that again," she
snarled.

"What did I do?"

"'Do you want a puppy?'" she mimicked. "To
a child, just asking is as good as a promise."

"I'll have to carry through on that promise,
won't I?"

Fury put a healthy glow on her high cheekbones.
"Then you'll keep it at your house and bring it with
you when you visit."

"I take it you don't like dogs."

"What I don't like is a man walking into my house and taking over as if he had every right."

Ian swallowed a chuckle. Shannon reminded him of a firecracker. When she exploded she looked even more beautiful. Her wide eyes glittered and passionate heat radiated from her.

"Don't you remember what it was like to have a pet?"

"We kids from the slums didn't have the luxury of pets," she rasped sarcastically.

Her arrow hit the mark. He'd never looked down on a person because of where he'd come from. "My comment in the lawyer's office was out of line."

"No. I should thank you. It helps to be reminded of my history, just in case I become complacent and forget."

"Forget what?"

"Forget what I don't want out of life." She spun around and marched into the kitchen, leaving him alone to figure out what she meant by her cryptic words.

Four

―――――

Ian raked his fingers through his hair. Shannon wasn't at all what he'd expected. He could understand how a childhood of poverty might have driven her sister into an affair with a wealthy older man. His father certainly wouldn't have discouraged a sexy young woman. Was she hoping to win that same kind of security?

If so, she played with a poker face. She had not contacted him once with regards to the company or the cash endowment left to her sister. His two offers of support money for Chelsea had been firmly refused. Where did she get the money to pay the bills on the house? "Freelance work" didn't sound as if it could provide a stable income for a single woman with a child.

The clang of metal striking metal and the subsequent muttered oath ended his curious train of thought. He went to the kitchen to check out the commotion.

"Are you staying for lunch?" she asked without looking up from her task of straightening the pots in the cupboard. Judging by her flat tone of voice she would rather have a root canal.

"If it's not too much trouble."

"And if I said it is?"

"I'd stay anyway."

She shook her head and exhaled a deep sigh. "Why did I know you were going to say that?"

"Great minds think alike?" he offered.

"More like the male mind is so predictable."

He stood directly behind her. Close enough to smell the lilac scent of her perfume, close enough to touch her although he didn't try. "Correct me if I'm wrong, but weren't you the one who suggested I spend time with Chelsea?"

"Yes," she mumbled. She turned and immediately pressed herself against the counter to avoid physical contact. He liked her discomfort and her undeniable awareness of him. "I didn't plan on having guests for lunch."

"I'll eat SpaghettiOs." He tried not to laugh at her grimace of distaste.

"I think I can do a little better than that."

"I'm sure I'd enjoy anything you'd give me."

If she caught his double entendre, she chose to ignore it. "I'd better go see what mischief Chelsea is getting into."

"I'll go." Before she could lodge a protest, he spun around and walked out of the kitchen.

Following the giggles, he found the child's room at the end of the hall. Chelsea was jumping on the canopy bed. A cloud of pink bed ruffles danced to the motion. When she saw him leaning in the doorway, she fell backward onto her bottom.

"Uh-oh." She slid to the floor and picked up the dress she had shed in favor of a sweatshirt.

He stepped inside the decidedly feminine bedroom. "What are you doing?"

"Nothing."

He picked up a pair of tiny green stretch pants from the back of the chair. "Are you supposed to put these on?"

She nodded.

"Well, hurry up," he said with a conspiratorial wink. "Aunt Shannon is waiting."

While Chelsea finished changing, he turned his back and gazed around the room. The white lacquer furniture and pink-and-white motif created a fairy-tale atmosphere. Pictures of unicorns and fairies adorned the walls. Shannon had gone all out to make the room a little girl's dream.

He leaned down to inspect a photograph of a younger Chelsea and her mother on top of the dresser.

"Mommy's in heaven." Chelsea's matter-of-fact statement was a testament to the resiliency of children, but it only served to renew his anger toward Wesley.

"I know."

"I have a birthday."

Ian wasn't big in the comfort department so her short attention span came as a relief. "When?"

She shrugged.

"How old are you going to be?"

She held up three fingers. "Free."

"What do you want?"

"A puppy."

Ian smiled, thankful that Shannon wasn't in earshot to hear Chelsea's request. "If I can't find a puppy, is there anything else you'd like?"

"A kitten."

"Oh, boy. You want to get me in trouble. Come on." He waved his hand to point to the door and was surprised when she clamped her small fingers over his. His stomach knotted. Her innocent acceptance of him when he had been so quick to dismiss her left him with the unfamiliar feeling of guilt.

Shannon pushed her glasses on top of her head and arched her back. Since the end of lunch she had locked herself in her room. If she was honest, she would acknowledge that the easy way Ian related to Chelsea left her feeling inadequate. But she preferred to lie, so she convinced herself that she had a lot of work to do. Besides, all men were babies so they naturally related better to children.

Now that she'd had her daily dose of male-bashing, her spirits lifted. She switched off the computer and walked around the room to stretch her legs. For a moment she enjoyed the silence until she realized the house was too quiet. Where was Chelsea?

She sprinted down the hall. When she saw her niece asleep on the sofa, relief ran through her. Well, what did you expect? she chided herself. Ian had more sense than to kidnap a child but he should have had enough consideration to let her know he was leaving. After covering Chelsea with the afghan and giving her a kiss, Shannon went to make herself a strong cup of coffee.

As she stepped into the kitchen, she caught the shadow of a movement in her peripheral vision. She whirled around and stumbled into the refrigerator behind her. A startled gasp stuck in her throat, threatening to choke her.

"Sorry," Ian said, but he didn't look contrite.

"Damn, you scared me." She drew in a large gulp of air. "I thought you'd left."

"Without thanking you? My mother raised me better than that." He stood next to her, resting his hand on the refrigerator, just above her shoulder.

The pounding in her chest slowed to merely double time as the scent of his musky aftershave began an all-out assault on her senses. The cool metal against her back contrasted with the heat coursing through her.

Adrenaline, she tried to convince herself.

Hormones, her mind taunted.

She tilted her head back to meet his challenging gaze. He might be melting her body with his proximity, but she didn't have to give him the satisfaction of knowing it.

"How long has Chelsea been asleep?"

"A few minutes. Why have you been hiding out in your room all afternoon?"

"I was giving you time alone with your sister."

"Because we might want to discuss something private like why Bugs Bunny is funnier than Goofy? Or maybe you believe in the sink-or-swim method of family relationships."

"You managed."

"And that really ticks you off, doesn't it? You hoped she'd hate me."

She shook her head in denial. The last thing she wanted was to start a war for the child's affection. She had lived through that with her own parents. She and Tiffany had come out the losers every time.

For Chelsea's sake Shannon wanted Ian to show a interest in the child's life. She only wished her niece had given Ian one-tenth the trouble *she* had experienced while trying to bond with Chelsea.

"If you'd relax a little, you wouldn't have so many problems with her," Ian said.

"Who says I have problems?"

"I saw for myself. Why did you get so tense over her refusing to eat lunch? Don't you realize that the bigger the issue you make the more she'll use it against you?"

"She's three years old, for goodness' sake, not some mastermind out to torment me."

"No, she's out for attention, and this is one way she gets your attention."

"Now I'm neglectful, too. I don't seem to have

one redeeming quality.'' She ducked under his arm and started to walk away.

Ian grasped her wrist firmly in his hand, forbidding her retreat. ''I didn't say that.'' He tugged her back to him. ''I doubt she's the first person who's ever wanted to have your undivided attention. And as for your redeeming qualities, I'd be happy to list them for you any time you'd like.''

''Well, I could pretty safely bet that nurturing, mothering and comforting aren't on the list.''

Ian grinned. Sexy, sensual, and arousing came to mind, along with a few other adjectives that would probably shock her out of her starched white blouse. Yes, she was uptight, but that only roused his desire to see her let loose.

She glanced down at the hand that still held her. ''Would you mind?''

''You are upset.''

''Because Chelsea got along with you?''

''Yes.''

''No. I got custody of a child who was starved for love. I spent six frustrating months building a trust with her so that just maybe she could have a normal and happy childhood and I'll be damned if I'll listen to you tell me everything I've done wrong.''

''I wasn't criticizing.''

''The hell you weren't.'' She jerked her hand free and folded her arms over her chest.

''It's apparent that you love her and she loves you. If she felt safe enough to spend the afternoon with me because she knew you were close by, then you're doing something right. I only meant that you should stop being so conscious of every move you make and loosen up a little.''

"Now I can add rigid to my long list of faults.''

He leaned against the counter and chuckled. "Did you major in guilt in school?''

Her eyes narrowed. "No. That's genetic. I learned it from my parents.''

"They taught you well.''

"People only feel guilty if they have something to feel guilty about. Do you?''

Ian shook his head. "Oh, no, you don't.'' He would not be drawn into this debate. Of course he felt guilty about his sister. How could he look at her trusting face with those huge blue eyes and not? However, he wasn't about to admit that and leave himself open to emotional manipulation.

"Are your parents still alive?'' he asked, to change the subject.

"My mother's in Palm Beach and my father's in L.A.''

"Two nice vacation spots to visit.''

"And three thousand miles apart. Too bad they didn't plan it that way when we were younger. It would have save a lot of heartache all the way around.''

Another survivor of the divorce wars, he thought. "And you just had the one sister?''

"Is this Twenty Questions?''

"You do have me at a disadvantage. I knew nothing about you or your family until last month.''

Shannon's upturned nose crinkled. "First of all,

I doubt you've ever let any woman close enough to have you at a disadvantage. Secondly, you knew my sister. She told me she'd met you.''

Right on both counts, he noted. ''So I made that much of an impression on your sister. What did she say about me?''

''I don't recall. I didn't pay attention when she talked about anything involving Wesley.'' She grimaced in distaste.

''You didn't approve?''

''What do you think? He was almost forty years older than her.''

He rolled his eyes. ''That didn't seem to bother your sister.''

She trembled and let out a sigh. ''Let's drop the conversation, Ian. It does no good to malign the dead.''

''You're right.'' While their lives would forever be entwined, the circumstances surrounding Chelsea's birth created a wall he couldn't get beyond. ''Instead we can work on arranging some sort of 'schedule for my visitation privileges.'''

She flopped into a chair at the kitchen table. ''All right. Maybe that came out a bit formal but it's not easy talking to you.''

''Why is that?''

''You put me on the defensive even though I don't owe you an explanation for anything I do. Do you treat your friends like that, or have I been singled out for that honor?''

Oddly, he'd never thought of himself as an aggressive person, yet that was how people perceived him. He didn't have friends, at least not in the way she meant. His college ties had long since unraveled. Although they still met for the occasional beer, their lives had taken different roads.

Round One to Shannon.

Until she'd asked about friends, he'd never thought of his life as being empty. Work was his mistress, but she wasn't there for him in the hours when he needed her most. The image of Shannon warming those long nights brought an uncustomary feeling of longing. And he liked the idea of seeing life through Chelsea's eyes. He hadn't realized that pure innocence still existed or that it could give comfort to someone as jaded as himself.

He frowned. Was he being fair? Shannon must be pleased with the deal since she'd laid down the terms. He would make sure that Chelsea never wanted for anything. All in all, this arrangement would suit him perfectly.

"Ian," she said. "If you plan to spend hours pondering the meaning of life, sit down. I'm getting a neck ache looking up at you."

He sat in the chair next to her. His thigh brushed against hers and she immediately straightened. He laughed. She glared.

"Three evenings a week," he said. "Would that be suitable?"

Her eyes expanded. "Three?"

"Not enough?" He deliberately misinterpreted her shock. "It's difficult to get up from the city, especially during the week. Okay. Full weekends and one evening."

"One day a week would be fine."

"For whom? This is for Chelsea, right? And a child needs time, quality and quantity. Don't let those experts fool you into thinking otherwise."

"Do you think this is a joke?" she snapped.

"No. I'm doing exactly what you asked of me—maintaining a relationship with my sister. Well, it takes time to build a relationship before I can maintain it."

Her face darkened angrily. "And let's not forget why. So you can have your precious company."

Ian held his temper in check. The company hadn't entered into his thoughts. He no longer cared if he bought Chelsea's shares as long as Adam got to run the company. So, why didn't he tell Shannon?

Because then he would have to explain why he had accepted her offer, and he wasn't sure of his motives.

"Whatever. My being here shouldn't interfere with your life."

Her laughter rang with disbelief. "Sure. And I suppose you have a bridge you'd like to sell me, too."

She shifted in the seat, easing her chair away from his. If he thought his presence wouldn't disrupt her life he was more dense than lead. However, reasoning with Ian would be a futile exercise. He was probably trying to get back at her for pushing him into this deal. If she was patient, he would get bored with the game after a month or so.

Why did that scenario bother her?

"Okay. Weekends and one evening. Except this Saturday isn't good. It's Chelsea's birthday and I'm having a small—"

"I'm not invited to my sister's party?" He feigned insult.

Shannon was about to explain that the party was for twenty children, all under the age of four. She smiled. "Of course you're welcome, Ian. The reservation is for one o'clock."

By his superior grin, he seemed to think he had outmaneuvered her. "I'll be here at twelve to drive."

After a couple hours at a Chuck E. Cheese's restaurant with a roomful of screaming kids, he would think twice before inviting himself anyplace again. "Fine."

He cocked his eyebrow skeptically. "Why are you being so agreeable?"

"Would it get me anywhere to argue with you?" she asked sweetly.

"I'm glad to see that you're wise enough to accept the inevitable."

Shannon was beginning to appreciate the family resemblance between Ian and Chelsea. The same tenacious determination to get their way. Identical powers of reasoning. Even that wounded frown they both pulled off with utter charm. They knew how to push her buttons.

Ian rose at the same time as Shannon. "Now that everything is settled, I have to get back to work," he said.

"You won't make it back to the city before

five." She lowered her gaze and silently cursed herself. She actually felt disappointed that he was leaving.

"After five is the busiest time in the freight business." He put his hand under her chin and raised her head. A seductive smile tugged at the corners of his mouth. "Unless there's a reason you'd like me to stay."

The man was as tempting as chocolate with none of the calories. Did she honestly believe she would be able to spend three days a week with him and still deny the inexplicable attraction between them? For her own sake she would have to try. She had the type of personality that was prone to compulsions. A workaholic, a chocoholic. She shuddered to think about the kind of obsession Ian would become.

When she had only herself to worry about, she could indulge her compulsions. Lately Shannon's desires took a back seat to what was in the best interest of the child. Chelsea's long-term relationship with Ian was more important than any "carnal fantasies" she might harbor toward him.

"No reason I can think of," she finally answered.

He laughed and released her. "Coward," he muttered on his way out the back door.

Shannon nodded. Better to let him think she was afraid than to let him know the truth. Ian had made it plain that he wanted her but at no time had he offered her anything in return.

Five

Ian pried another set of sticky hands off his jeans. He handed the young boy some game tokens. For the next fifteen seconds he had a reprieve, until the others caught on that he was the one holding the golden coins. Shannon watched him from across the room, looking mighty pleased with herself. With a Barbie party hat on her head and a broad grin lighting up her face, she sat back and relished his predicament.

When she had told him they were going for pizza he'd envisioned a small parlor with a light Italian menu. Instead he got a bizarre video palace with mechanical musicians and a person dressed up in a rodent costume. The level of noise coming from the packs of children was enough to cause hearing loss.

That's what he got for trying to take over, he

thought. He should have known there was a reason Shannon had allowed him to assume control the moment he had arrived at her house. While he had the job of chasing around after twenty children, she lounged around a table with the parents and enjoyed the party. As he handed out another token, he vowed he would never again make the mistake of underestimating Shannon.

Shannon took a sip of her soda and relaxed in the seat. The day was not the fiasco she'd imagined and grudgingly she admitted Ian was the reason. His pied piper ability to keep the children entertained took the pressure off her. Of course, no favor came without a price and hers was being forced to endure Wendy's interfering questions and droll grins.

"What's the matter with you, girl?" Wendy asked. "He's under fifty, has all his teeth and he's good with kids. What more could you ask for in a man?"

"Get a life," Shannon mumbled.

"He hasn't taken his eyes off you."

"That's a glare of scorn in case you hadn't noticed."

Wendy shook her head. "You're hopeless."

"Then give up. He's Chelsea's big brother. Nothing more."

She stood. "There's no talking to you. I'll have to talk to Ian."

"Don't you dare." Shannon sprang to her feet.

By the time she had gotten around the long table,

a hostess stopped her to let her know that the pizza was ready. While Shannon rounded up the children, she could only imagine what joke Ian was sharing with her friend. And she couldn't understand why she felt jealous to see them laughing together when she vehemently denied any interest in him.

With the children sitting down to eat their lunch, Ian collapsed in a chair in the corner for a moment of solitude. No wonder Shannon didn't have time to hold down more than a part-time job. Chelsea was a full-time job. He chuckled. Shannon had set him up today and he couldn't honestly blame her after the condescending way he had spoken to her. Not that he would admit as much. She took too much pleasure in his exhaustion for him to let her know she had been right.

Even now, as she walked toward him, he noticed the I-got-you-good smile brightening her entire face. A jade green pantsuit clung to her rounded curves and a silver belt emphasized her narrow waist. Her tongue absently moistened her full red lips. All in all, he would guess she wanted to add a helping of torment to his earlier pain and suffering.

"You're not wearing your Power Rangers hat," she said.

"My head's too big. The elastic broke."

She sat in the chair next to him and handed him a slice of pizza. "That's no surprise. So, was the day everything you thought it would be?"

"Beyond my expectations."

"Good. I was afraid you would feel out of place."

He leaned in closer to savor the floral scent of her perfume, feel the warmth of her body only inches from him. What she did to him with her mere nearness, many women had not been able to accomplish with their best efforts. He swallowed hard.

"So what's the plan for the rest of the day?" he asked.

Her soft laughter drifted over his neck. "You're up for more?"

"Now that's a loaded question."

Confusion flashed in her eyes but her expression quickly changed to one of embarrassed surprise. A hot flush stained her cheeks and she shyly gazed around to make sure no one was in earshot. "You're incredible," she mumbled through clenched teeth.

"That's what I've been trying to tell you."

"A man who sings his own praises has a fan club of one."

"According to your friend, you're not a woman who is drawn to the shy and meek."

"Well, I wouldn't put too much faith in anything Wendy had to say. She thinks that the very fact you have a pulse is reason enough to—" She cut off her words abruptly.

He dipped his head to see her lowered face. "Reason enough to what?"

"Forget it. I have to collect Chelsea's presents. The party is nearly over."

He cupped his hand over her thigh to keep her from vaulting out of the chair. "We will finish this discussion." She removed his hand and rose.

Ian watched her swift retreat with amusement. He was getting to her. No more than she had gotten to him. He spent most of his waking hours distracted by thoughts of Shannon. And what thoughts he was having!

He needed to alleviate this fevered preoccupation with her and he knew only two ways to accomplish that. One, he could give up and return to his solitary way of life before he got in too deep. Or he could put aside his inherent distrust, open his mind to the possibility of a long-term relationship and take the plunge.

Just the thought caused his stomach muscles to contract painfully. There had to be a middle ground between the two.

Shannon arranged the brightly wrapped packages on the kitchen table. Chelsea had fallen asleep on the ride home, but any minute she would awaken and want to open the gifts from the party. Shannon glanced at her watch. Ian had been gone nearly an hour. Although she assured him that Chelsea wouldn't notice, he had still insisted on going to the mall to pick up a present for her. No dogs, she had warned him, but where Ian was concerned, Shannon didn't necessarily believe he would respect her wishes.

She curled up in the corner of the sofa and laid her head back to stare at the ceiling. Ian was a hard man to understand. One minute he had exuded seductive charm and the next she could have been a statue for all the interest he had shown her. Then again, her own emotions were none too clear. She felt edgy when he made a pass and insulted when he didn't. Talk about sending out mixed signals.

Perhaps she should figure out what she wanted. No, she knew. She wanted some pure, unadulterated, knock-your-socks-off sex. Unfortunately, she wasn't the kind of person who could indulge in a casual affair for the hell of it and walk away with her emotions intact. Where would that leave Chelsea when Ian lost interest in Shannon?

By the time Ian returned she had convinced herself that a relationship with him was out of the question. He walked in the front door. Her heart beat a little faster. His black jeans and black-and-white flannel shirt molded his well-toned body. He strode across the room with the confidence of a man who knew he was being admired.

"We have to talk later," he warned, then continued down the hall to his sister's room.

Did he think she was going somewhere? She lived here—a fact he seemed to overlook when he walked into her house without pausing to knock.

Minutes later he returned with Chelsea in his arms.

The child beamed with happiness. "Ian buyed me a present."

Shannon smiled back. "I know. And it better not require walking three times a day."

Chelsea wrinkled her button nose in confusion.

Ian plopped her down next to Shannon and sprinted outside. He returned with a large box. As he placed it on the coffee table, Chelsea scooted off the sofa to open her present.

"Kitty," Chelsea shrieked in delight.

"You didn't," was all Shannon could manage as her niece lifted the white ball of fur into her arms. *He's a dead man. I'm going to choke the life out of him with my bare hands.* "Don't squeeze him too tight, Chels."

"What do you think?" Ian asked proudly. "She likes it, huh?"

"I'll answer that later. When there are no witnesses and I have access to a carving knife," she muttered with syrupy sweetness.

As Chelsea cuddled the animal closer, Shannon knew any hope of returning the pet was lost.

"Why don't you show him your room, squirt?" Ian waited for the child to disappear before continuing. "You said no dog. I didn't get a dog. A pet teaches responsibility."

"Since I'll be the one who feeds it, changes the litter box and runs around trying to stop the little beast from shredding my furniture, should I assume that you think I need to learn more responsibility? What, raising your father's child isn't enough?"

Ian's eyes darkened with anger.

She stopped and took a deep breath. "I didn't mean that the way it sounded. You should have asked me first."

He towered over her, glaring down his long, autocratic nose. "You would have said no."

"You're damn right I would."

"I rest my case." Tension seeped from the pores of his rigid body. "And if raising Wesley's child is too much for you, why won't you accept financial help?"

"Because not every woman in the world is out to get the Bradford fortune. I, for one, don't need that kind of help, or the suspicions that would always be attached to it."

Ian paced the room. Talking to Shannon was an exercise in frustration. She had more pride than sense. "Did it occur to you that I *want* to contribute toward Chelsea's upbringing?"

She stared pensively as if judging the sincerity of his words. "If you really want to, that's fine. But I'll never ask you for anything."

Her refusal to ask him for help forced him to reevaluate the way he dealt with her. He had no hold over her, save her desire for him to visit his sister. Even though she apparently thought him to be without conscience, he wouldn't use the child as leverage. "Good. The money issue is settled. Do you want me to take the kitten back to the store?"

"So that you can be the heroic big brother and I'm the evil witch aunt? Forget it." Shannon stood and straightened the pillows on the sofa.

Apparently she wasn't happy with his choice of gift. She wanted him to be involved in the child's life. Did he have to run every decision past her first?

"I won't do anything without asking your permission again."

A hint of a smile softened her features. "Don't compound the problem by lying. You'll do whatever the hell you want. Just think before you make a decision that makes more work for me."

"Deal." He offered his hand and, trusting soul that she was, she took it. With a tug, he had her flush against his body.

"What are you doing?"

"Sealing our pact." While his fingers cupped her waist, she pressed her palms against his chest.

"Don't."

"Why?"

"Just because I said the cat could stay doesn't mean I'm not mad at you."

"You'll get over it." He started to lower his head.

"Chelsea will be back any second."

As if on cue the child came flying down the hall two steps behind a cloud of white fluff. Before Shannon could react, the kitten clawed its way up the leg of her silk pantsuit. She let out a startled cry of pain. Her eyes filled with tears and her expression turned thunderous.

Chelsea clapped her hands and giggled in delight. "Give me. Give me."

Ian tried to pry the animal from the spot it had dug into on Shannon's chest. She winced. He couldn't blame the kitten for holding on. If he had his hands there he wouldn't want to let go, either.

"Monday morning this ferocious beast is getting declawed." She grabbed the furball by the scruff of its neck and turned it loose on the floor. As she stood again, he saw the two red stains on her blouse.

"You're bleeding," he whispered.

"Aunt Shane have a boo-boo," Chelsea said, the worry clearly reflected in her small face.

Shannon sent the child a soothing smile. "Only a little one."

"Kiss the boo-boo?"

"I will," Ian gladly volunteered.

"Don't you have someplace to be? Some other women you can torment?"

"My weekends belong to you and Chelsea."

"Oh, joy."

He ignored her less-than-enthusiastic reply. "Why don't we open the rest of your presents, Chelsea, and Aunt Shane can fix her *boo-boo*."

"'Kay." She nodded but her eyes remained fixed on the growing red stain.

"Go on," Shannon said. "I'll change and be right back. Start without me."

Ian shrugged an apology. He had a good mind to ring the neck of the hair ball himself. In the store window, the kitten had looked the picture of gentle innocence. When would he learn that things weren't always what they seemed?

Shannon wrapped a towel around her body and stepped out of the shower. She opened the door a crack. Chelsea's bubbly voice drifted down the hall. Obviously, she enjoyed her brother's company.

And surprisingly, Ian played his role of sibling with patience and genuine affection. That still didn't let him off the hook for bringing an animal into the house.

Grabbing a comb, Shannon smoothed the tangles from her hair. When she finished, she bent to check a few minor scratches on her leg. The door creaked and she bolted upright. A breath caught in her throat. She folded her arms across her chest to hold the towel in place as Ian stepped inside the small bathroom.

"Don't you believe in knocking?"

"You didn't close the door."

She shook her head and grumbled a few less-than-ladylike comments under her breath. "Where's Chelsea?"

"Watching *The Lion King*."

Her toes wiggled in a puddle of water. "This isn't a good time for a chat."

"How's the…" He gestured toward her chest.

"They weren't too bad."

"Let me see."

"Are you a doctor?"

"I'll play doctor if you want." His seductive grin jump-started her pulse.

She had to admire his persistence, even if his presumptuousness left something to be desired. "I can take care of it myself."

"No way. I brought the beast into the house. I'm responsible for the damages. Where is the antiseptic? In the medicine cabinet?" Before she could stop him he opened the left-side door. If she didn't already feel awkward enough, her birth control pills

and feminine hygiene products were the only items
on the shelf.

"Do you mind?" she snapped, and slid the mirror across the cabinet.

"No. I don't mind." He pulled a tube of cream
from the right-hand shelf and read the label. "Let
me see those scratches."

She put up resistance as he tried to move her
hands.

"I assure you my interest is purely clinical," he
said.

"Liar." She lowered her hands to her waist, determined to ignore the intimacy of his actions. The
two lesions fell across the swell of her breasts. After
squeezing a dollop of antibiotic cream on his
thumb, he covered the area in a tender stroking motion.

Her heart pounded in her chest. So much for ignoring him. She wondered if he felt the rapid ca-
dence, too. Closing her eyes, she rested against the
counter for support as a wave of pleasure surged
through her.

His hand slipped inside the towel and worked
around to her back, bringing her closer. She should
be outraged or at least embarrassed by the liberties
he was taking. Instead she snuggled closer and
turned her face up to him.

His mouth covered hers. His tongue traced the
outline of her lips before plunging inside. She inhaled deeply. He tasted sweet. The longing for release rose in her like a fire. She pressed against him,
feeling the hard evidence of his own desire.

As he covered her face, her neck, her shoulder in moist kisses, she could do little more than hold on to him. She had heard the expression "legs turned to jelly" before, but she had never fully appreciated the analogy until now. A whirlpool of need threatened to pull her into the swirling depths.

With her last ounce of self-control, she grabbed the flannel of his shirt and wedged some distance between them. "Ian. Stop."

He gazed at her, breathless and confused. "Don't tell me you didn't want me."

"I don't lie."

"Then what's wrong?"

"We have about two more minutes before Chelsea's attention span begins to wander and she comes looking for us." Shannon straightened her towel and tried to look dignified in light of her wanton behavior. "And frankly, if you plan to finish in less than two minutes, I'm not too interested in what you're offering."

He roared with laughter. "I see the problem. What time does she go to sleep?"

"About five minutes before I do."

"I can keep you awake," he muttered.

She poked her finger playfully into his chest. "Don't count on it. There's nothing I enjoy more than my sleep."

"I'll be changing your opinion on that soon."

"Your modesty is touching." She slipped around him and scooted out the door. She knew he was right, but damn it, she would make him work a lot harder before she gave in.

Six

On Sunday morning Ian woke early. It was not difficult considering he had spent the night in a reclining chair. When he had planted himself there last night he had figured Shannon would get back to him once she had Chelsea settled for the night. Unfortunately, his sister, running on a sugar rush from her birthday cake, had stayed awake even after her aunt had drifted off.

Along with the aches from his awkward sleeping position, he had the added ache of frustration. He had thought about—hell, he'd dreamed about the moment he would get Shannon alone again. It had been a long time since he had wanted a woman as much as he wanted her. That might explain why he had spent the night in a chair instead of going back to the city.

He stretched and brought his chair into the upright position. The faint sound of a gasp surprised him. Chelsea was kneeling on the sofa, staring at him. Her blue eyes widened and she smiled.

"Aunt Shane," she bellowed at a blood-curdling pitch. "Ian waked up."

Footsteps padded down the hall. Shannon entered the room and nodded. Dressed in shorts and a college sweatshirt she looked like a coed on summer break. "You know, we do have a guest room. Next time you invite yourself to spend the night you might want to try it."

He raised his eyebrow invitingly. "I had a different bed in mind."

She ignored his comment and began picking up the trail of toys around the room.

"I can watch Simba now?" Chelsea asked.

Shannon shook her head. "After breakfast."

Chelsea's bottom lip trembled and tears welled up in her eyes. She sniffed, then began to cry in earnest.

Ian didn't deal well with weeping females of any age. "What's the difference if—"

"Stay out of this," Shannon warned.

When he opened his mouth, she waved him into the kitchen. Giving Chelsea an apologetic shrug, he followed Shannon.

Obviously, she wasn't a morning person. She shot him an angry glare but kept her voice low as she spoke. "When you want to contradict me, do it in private."

"Are you hung over on birthday cake? It's only a movie."

"That's not the point. She's not allowed to watch television before breakfast. She has to be taught some rules and we have to be consistent."

"That's not my job."

"We're the closest thing she's got to parents. If you're part of her life, it *is* your job. If you're not interested, let me know now."

The idea that Chelsea might think of him as a father figure had a sobering effect. He had envisioned himself as more of a benevolent uncle.

He watched as Shannon made a pot of coffee and laid out two cups. She had given him the perfect opportunity to back out of their deal. After all, what kind of role model would he make for a child? He thought about Shannon raising Chelsea alone or, worse, with some other man in their lives. Refusing to acknowledge the tightening in his stomach as jealousy, he raised his shoulders in a casual acceptance of her terms.

"Fine. I'll...ahh." A set of sharp claws bearing down on his bare foot cut off his reply. He bent and picked up the kitten. "Listen, Snowball. You've already made enough trouble for me."

"Not nearly as much as you deserve," Shannon muttered. "And as long as we're setting down the rules and regulations of the house, you can feed *Snowball* his smelly cat food right after you clean up the mess he made when he missed the litter box."

"Why me?"

"You brought him into the house." She ran her finger along the collar of his shirt and smiled. "Set an example and teach your sister some responsibility."

"You're cruel."

She expelled a puff of air. "You didn't spend the night kicking him off your bed."

He raised the kitten in the air. "You little devil. I'm envious."

"No need to be. I'd be more than happy to land my foot in your rump."

He grinned. "If you're into kinky, I prefer something with handcuffs."

She yanked a paper towel off the holder and handed it to him. "Clean."

"Silk scarves?"

"Now!"

"Yes, Aunt Shane."

He muttered several expletives while he took on the thankless task. Is this what his life had come to? Cleaning cat...mess and trying to ignore a three-year-old's temper tantrum? Why hadn't he stayed in New York and sent the checks as he had planned?

The answer stood three feet away, laughing at his grimace of disgust.

"I'm glad you're amused," he muttered.

"What do you want for breakfast?"

"Who can eat after that?"

"It will pass. Bacon and eggs or pancakes?"

He leaned against the wall and crossed his arms casually over his chest. "I imagined you would be making me breakfast under slightly different circumstances.''

Shannon wriggled her nose. ''Under the circumstances you mean, *you'd* be making *me* breakfast.''

''Is that right?'' He reached for her but she side-stepped his hand.

''Chelsea's just in the next room.''

''What are you going to do when you can't use Chelsea as an excuse?''

''I don't know. Probably give in.''

''Oh.'' He took a mug from the counter and filled it to the brim with coffee. ''Does Chelsea have a favorite baby-sitter?''

''That was subtle, Ian.'' She opened the refrigerator door and bent to pick through the contents. Her long legs disappeared under the edge of the shorts that molded her rounded bottom. A heat wave descended over the kitchen.

He got the impression she knew exactly where he was staring as she swayed her hips in time to a song she softly hummed. To think he had once wondered if she gave as good as she got. She didn't get mad. Nor was she content with only getting even. She paid him back in spades.

''I have to go through Wesley's house. I thought maybe…''

She gazed up at him suspiciously. ''You thought what?''

''I wondered if you might want to pick out a few things for Chelsea. He was her father…''

''She never knew him.''

''That's probably to her benefit. However, I don't

have any use for the stuff, so before it's auctioned off, I thought you might take a trip there with me.''

''I don't know.''

''Would it really hurt Chelsea to let her think her father wasn't all bad?''

Shannon's surprise reflected his own shock. Although he had originally offered as a ploy to have time alone with her, his intentions were sincere. Ian wasn't defending his cold, indifferent father but rather seeking to spare Chelsea from the knowledge that had clouded so many of his own perceptions as an adult.

''What do you say?'' he asked.

She hesitated before giving her reluctant answer. ''I guess so. When?''

''You tell me.''

''I have a meeting in the city on Tuesday. I guess I could ask Wendy to keep her all day and I'll meet you somewhere.''

He grinned and a sense of calm fell over him. He had avoided his father's house since the funeral and even in the years before Wesley's death. Letting Chelsea have the artwork and collectibles seemed appropriate. He could finally close a bitter chapter in his life. That he was conceivably opening a new chapter was something he wouldn't contemplate.

Shannon waited until Ian's car turned the corner. Then, taking Chelsea's hand, she walked across the soft carpet of grass to Wendy's house. The fragrant peonies scented the early summer air. Chelsea ran ahead to join her friend Anna on the swing set in the backyard.

Wendy met her at the door with a cup of coffee in hand. "Did you have a nice weekend?"

Shannon chose a seat that gave her a view of the children. "I survived the party."

Her friend smiled wryly. "You had great help."

"Yes, Chelsea's brother was helpful."

"Chelsea's brother," Wendy repeated. "And I suppose that was just a devoted nephew bidding farewell to his favorite aunt when he planted that goodbye kiss on you."

Shannon felt her cheeks flame, adding to the heat wave Ian had showered over her before his departure. "Were you watching?"

"You were right out there on the street. I happened to be looking out the living room window."

"Don't read too much into a friendly kiss." She sipped her coffee.

"Okay. Deny if you must."

"Can you take Chelsea on Tuesday? I might be late."

"She and Anna can have a slumber party. Are you meeting Ian?"

Shannon furrowed her brows. "Why would you assume that?"

Wendy raked her fingers through her mop of curls. "You don't meet with clients after hours. If you're going to be late, a man is involved."

"All right, Sherlock. You win." Shannon tossed her hands up in guilty surrender. "Yes, I'm meeting with Ian."

"Business or pleasure?"

"I'm not sure."

"Why?"

"Because I don't know if I can handle what he's offering. Or more accurately, what he's not offering. Sex isn't enough."

"Oh, Shannon. No man, my own dear husband included—" Wendy gestured toward the living room, where her exhausted spouse was sleeping in front of the television "—enters a relationship with the intention of making a commitment. Actually, they fight it."

"But some men can be persuaded."

"Any man can, with the right argument. Hey, you might find you're the one who loses interest. You can't give up on having a relationship because you might get hurt."

"I'm going, aren't I?" Shannon asked.

"And expecting the worst," her friend accused.

A delightful tingle ran along her spine. "Not completely."

She had no doubt that an affair with Ian would have many pleasurable benefits. Would they be enough to outweigh the inevitable heartache that would follow one day? He wasn't looking for permanency. She wasn't even sure he was considering long-term. However, he did want her and it had been a long time since anyone had wanted her in that way.

Ian led Shannon into the large Tudor house. The air smelled stale. A hollow echo followed their footsteps down the corridor to the study. He couldn't remember how long it had been since he had set foot in his father's house. At least five years, maybe more.

He hadn't moved in the same circles as his father, a fact that was no accident. Ian made sure he avoided Wesley whenever possible. On the few occasions, weddings and funerals mostly, when they'd had to be in the same place, they'd squared off on opposite sides of the room.

Just the house brought back a multitude of bad memories. When he was younger, he had been forced to spend every other weekend with his father as mandated by the terms of his parents' divorce. Afterward he would return to his grandfather's home to face the kindly man who had lost his company due to Wesley's conniving. Ian's childhood guilt had grown into deep anger and cynicism.

"Nice house." Shannon's husky voice reminded him that he wasn't alone.

Relegating the memories to the corner of his heart long ago closed off to the world, he turned his attention to his companion. Her tailored business suit gave her a standoffish air and he realized that for Shannon, clothes were a matter of attitude rather than a fashion statement.

"What were you expecting?"

She wrinkled her nose in distaste. "You don't want to know."

"Sure I do."

"Mirrors on the ceiling. Strobe lights with dimmer switches."

"A mechanical fold-out bed and a healthy supply of Spanish Fly?" Ian added.

"Something like that," she mumbled.

He grinned at the stereotypical image that hadn't been far off the mark. "He had an apartment in the city for his affairs. The house was for business purposes. He never mixed the two."

"How professional of him." Sarcasm hardened her words.

"Yeah. He was a real upstanding guy."

She tilted her head slightly and frowned. "I'm sorry. I have no right to judge. I met him only once in the two years he…dated Tiffany."

"Two years? She lasted longer than most."

If he meant to make her feel better, he'd failed. The mention of her sister's affair opened a barely healed wound.

She gave her attention to the wall of cherrywood shelves. This was not the ordinary bric-a-brac that most people saved from vacations and family events. From ivory figurines and lead crystal pieces to paintings and carvings that many collectors would give their eyeteeth to own, Wesley had amassed a tidy fortune in artwork.

"He liked nice things," she noted.

"He liked to impress clients. It's easier to convince people you know what you're doing if you appear to profit from your knowledge. Very important in the investment field."

Shannon understood that concept. She didn't choose to constrict herself in the severe business suits that cost more than a week's salary for most people. That was the price of doing business in the city.

"Do you see anything you like?" he asked.

"Me?"

"For Chelsea." Ian seemed distracted. From the moment he had met her at the café and begun the journey to Connecticut, he had been quiet and withdrawn. She wasn't sure of his mood and she didn't want to say anything that might set him off.

"Why don't you choose something for her?"

"We'll just box it all up. When she's older, she can sell what she doesn't want."

"Do you have any idea what this stuff is worth?" she said without thinking. Ian tensed and shot her a stony glare. "Of course you do," she added apologetically. "Don't you want to save it?"

"Am I more entitled than Chelsea? I got his money as well as the house and half the company. She can have the rest."

"I guess." Shannon twisted her fingers together nervously. While she understood how emotional the visit must be for him, she had no wish to get caught in the cross fire of his love-hate relationship with his father. "It makes me feel awkward."

"Oh, forget it. I've decided. The stuff belongs to Chelsea. End of discussion."

"Don't get mad because I'm not the gold digger you expected."

His eyes widened in surprise. "Is that what this is all about? If I believed you would take something from a child for yourself, you wouldn't be here."

"Why, thanks for that resounding endorsement of my character."

Ian shoved his hands into his pockets and shrugged. "Sorry. It's this place."

"Then let's go."

"What?"

"You said the place makes you uncomfortable. We don't have to stay."

"I didn't say that."

Although he seemed determined to deny any feelings, Ian was obviously haunted by his past. His resentment toward his father remained unresolved, even in death.

"Is there a point to staying? We don't have any boxes with us. Have the stuff packed and sent whenever you want."

She closed her fingers over his rigid arm. For a long moment he seemed to stare right through her. He shook his head and exhaled slowly. His smile returned and the ghosts disappeared.

"You're right. Let's go. Where?"

She lowered her head. "What did you have in mind?"

He placed his hands on her waist and eased her closer. "What did *you* have in mind?"

Shannon cupped her hands over his shoulders to keep her balance. His body, still stiff with the earlier tension, relaxed as she nuzzled closer. "You first."

"Are you hungry?"

"A little."

"Chinese take-out?"

She raised her shoulders. "They don't have good take-out in Walton."

"But they do in the city."

She pressed her body flush against his, reveling in the way his hard muscles fit her rounder curves. "Any place in particular?"

A deep groan vibrated in his chest. "Right up the street from my apartment."

"That sounds very convenient." Her conscience tried to warn her of the possible dangers ahead, but her body had stopped listening to her mind.

Ian made her feel things she didn't understand but couldn't resist. She knew next to nothing about him. He didn't verbalize his emotions but she believed that somewhere, buried beneath the distrust, was a man worth knowing. How could she get below the surface?

"We better leave now or I won't be able to wait until we get back to the city," he muttered in her ear.

He wanted her and heaven knew she wanted him more than her next breath. Was it enough? She wouldn't know the answer until it was too late to save herself because she didn't have the willpower or the desire to say no.

Seven

Shannon popped the last bite of shrimp toast into her mouth. The woman had a healthy appetite, Ian noted. When they had arrived at the apartment, he had offered her an old college sweatshirt to change into. With grateful thanks, she had shed her constricting business suit and the rigid attitude that went along with it. Sitting cross-legged on the floor, with her hair falling freely about her shoulders, she presented a sensual picture that had dulled his taste for Lin Fung's famous Lobster Cantonese. Part of her master plan, he discovered, for she had eaten most of his food as well as her own.

During the course of dinner she played the part of a sexy vixen to the hilt. Watching her eat was an erotic pleasure in itself. She attacked her food with unbridled passion. He only hoped she would save one half her enthusiasm for him. She ran her tongue across her lips, savoring the last taste with a longing sigh. His jeans seemed to shrink in the ensuing heat. He extended his legs under the coffee table to relieve the pressure, but the only true relief was sitting directly across from him.

He tapped his foot against her bare thigh. "Still hungry?"

"No."

"Well, I am."

She crawled around the table, her graceful, feline movements arousing him further. From the opening at the V-neck of the sweatshirt he could see the swells of her breasts. "I suppose since I ate all your dinner I should at least offer you some dessert."

"At the very least."

"Is that right?" She arched her delicate eyebrow. "And I thought you fed me out of the goodness of your heart. Did you really think I could be had for a couple of egg rolls?"

His lips curved down in a frown. "I'm not in the mood for games."

She straightened and sat back on her heels. "There's a difference between teasing and playing games, Ian. I knew what I was getting into when I accepted your invitation."

"I just want to make sure we both understand the rules. We are two reasonably intelligent people entering into a mature relationship with no strings attached."

"Just two consenting adults indulging in a romantic interlude. Nothing heavy or serious," she added.

Ian grinned and relaxed against the back of the leather sofa. "Right."

Shannon blew a wisp of bangs off her forehead. "Damn, Ian. You sure know how to kill a mood."

His jaw dropped. "What did I say?"

"While I'm wondering how to get you out of your clothes you're worried that I might be trying to get into your pockets. I can't tell you what a turn-on that is." Sarcasm resonated in her husky voice.

"You're the one who told me to be honest."

"I'm not looking to land myself a husband. After watching my parents indulge in a ten-year bout of tug-of-war using their kids as the rope, I can honestly say marriage is not on my mind. But I don't do one-night stands, either."

"Neither do I." One night wouldn't be enough to get her out of his system. That chilling thought had cost him sleep in the past few nights. Had he been so completely offensive because he subconsciously wanted to push her away? If so, why was she still here?

He reached for her but she ducked and deftly eluded his grasp. "No way. Now you'll have to make an effort."

Grabbing the empty food cartons from the glass table, Shannon dashed into the galley kitchen. Ian remained in his spot on the living room floor. He was a difficult man to understand. Whenever he came remotely close to revealing his tender side, he threw up a granite barricade that effectively shut her out. His one Achilles' heel was Chelsea, but Shannon suspected he hadn't given in to those emotions without a strong internal struggle.

Ian was a mass of contradictions. A man equally as comfortable in a designer suit or faded blue jeans. His apartment was a perfect reflection of his personality. Stark white walls and black furniture. Brass accents added the only touch of color to the place. Although it was spacious by New York City standards, she had expected his home to be a more conspicuous display of his wealthy background.

As she stood at the sink to wash the few dishes, he came up behind her. Her elbows deep in soapsuds, she couldn't escape before he pinned her to the counter with his body. Worn denim brushed against her bare legs. He snaked his arms around her and splayed his hands over her stomach.

"That's cheating," she said on a sharp intake of air.

Ian's chuckle fanned her neck. "I told you I don't like games. But if I have to, I play to win."

She closed her eyes. Why bother fighting what they both knew she wanted? She nestled herself against his solid body and exhaled a sigh of contentment.

The rhythm of his heartbeat played softly against her ear. She waited for his next move but he just held her as if he had all the time in the world. His determination to keep the pace slow had the opposite effect. She wanted more and she wanted it now!

As she reached for the bottom of the sweatshirt,

he caught her wrists. "Are you in some kind of hurry?"

"No," she lied, but the slight quiver in her voice revealed the truth.

"Good things come to those who wait." A trace of laughter punctuated his words. The man was too cocky for his own good.

"He who hesitates is lost."

"I stand warned." He bunched the fleece fabric in his grasp and slowly pulled the shirt over her head.

She trembled, half from the sudden rush of cool air and half with anticipation.

He eased her back into the warmth of his arms. His rippling chest muscles flexed as he pulled her closer. He felt too good. She could get used to him but her mind warned her not to expect too much. The strength of his embrace blanketed her with a feeling of safety and washed away the last remaining doubts.

His chin nuzzled the side of her cheek. He peppered a trail of kisses along her shoulder and neck.

She wanted to see his face. She tried to turn but he held her firmly against him.

"I'm not finished here yet." His hands outlined the contours of her body, lingering just long enough to arouse before moving on. Anticipation rose to fevered heights. She wriggled against him. The evidence of his own desire pressed against her back, scorching her in its intensity. At least she wasn't the only one who was impatient.

He treated one of her ears to a sprinkling of moist

kisses. Her body responded by pricking all her nerve endings to attention. "Ian?"

"Mmm." His primal groan reverberated through her.

"You win the game. Okay?"

"I've only just begun to play," he muttered in her ear. With practiced ease, he released the front catch of her bra. He turned her around to face him. His heated gaze took her breath away. "Beautiful."

Apprehension made her stomach flutter. Ian's brand of lovemaking was like nothing she'd experienced before. For what she would gain, she knew she would inevitably lose a piece of herself. She had never been willing to give that power to any man, let alone a man who stated up front that he planned to walk away with his heart intact.

Ian was either oblivious to her misgivings or determined to overcome them. Using his tongue, he traced a line from her shoulder to her breast. He took the pebbled nipple into his mouth and sucked with a greedy hunger that obliterated all conscious thought from her mind. She buried her fingers into his silky hair. The need coursing through her was too much to fight against.

He dropped to his knees. The last of her clothing fell to the floor. He cupped her buttocks in his palms and inched her forward. His tongue circled her navel.

"Ian." She barely recognized the anguished moan as her own.

At the sound of his name hovering on her lips, Ian glanced up. Although she seemed long beyond the point of caring, she deserved better than a roll on the kitchen floor. In a fluid movement that caused her to gasp, he came to his feet and scooped her up into his arms. Her golden eyes held his gaze. She turned her face up to kiss him.

On the walk to the bedroom, he relied on memory to find his way. As he broke away to put her on the bed, she let out a muffled groan.

Flushed with desire, she lay her head back on the pillow and watched him undress. A halo of auburn hair framed her face. The unexpected need to possess her filled him. He knelt before her. Her skin was smooth and hot, her hands eager and impatient as she reached for him.

"Not yet," he whispered. His control was hanging by a thread. Her touch would send him over the edge before he got started.

First with his hand, then his mouth, he explored her body. She writhed beneath him as he tasted and teased. When his mouth moved to the downy soft mound between her thighs, her body went rigid.

"No."

He met her startled gaze. "Do you trust me?"

She nodded slowly.

"Then don't be afraid. You're going to like this." He was obviously bringing her into unfamiliar territory, returning the advantage to him once again. He took each move slow, giving her time to acclimate to the intimacy they were sharing.

Her fingers clutched the fabric of the bedspread in a death grip. She trembled and opened up to him, removing her last barrier of resistance. He caressed her inner thigh with fluid movements, bringing his fingers higher to part the folds of skin and expose the tiny pink nub at the center.

She let out a small cry.

"Do you want me to stop?" he asked, although he planned to persuade her otherwise. He had waited too long to see her come apart to give her time to regroup.

She shook her head and arched her hips upward.

Encouraged by her response, he sucked on the pulsing nub. Her taste was pure nectar, her uninhibited moaning, music. Although he thought he might explode with the force of his own desire, he couldn't stop. Her pleasure became his pleasure. Her climax more important than his own. Desire to satisfy his partner was a new and enlightening experience.

"Please." Her word was lost in a sob.

"Soon," he promised.

Moisture poured from her thick and hot. She clenched reflexively around his probing finger. More than ready, she was lost in a frenzy. He reached into the bedside table and grabbed a foil packet. Her fingernails stroked his back, beckoning him with their soft drumming. When he took too long, she playfully pinched his side to get his attention.

As she reached for him again, he came to her. Her body shuddered with shock waves as he entered. She closed around him, tangling him in a web of heat. Her nails dug into the flesh of his back.

He moved inside her, slowly at first, but building

with fevered intensity as she adjusted to accommodate all of him. He filled her over and over, each time testing what remained of his self-control.

She held him as if she were afraid he might try to leave. Smiling, he touched his mouth to hers. Joined so completely with her, he felt the exact moment of her release. Silent tears spilled from her glazed eyes. He licked them, savoring the salty taste. Only then did he allow himself the pleasure of the same, exhilarating climax.

Shannon cuddled against Ian and closed her eyes. She draped her arm across his waist, the warmth of his flesh acting like a sedative. Her body still tingled with contentment. As the last afterglow began to fade, the first twinges of reality set in.

Ian moved restlessly next to her, his naked body growing tense. "Tired?" he asked.

"A bit."

He seemed to heave a sigh of relief. "Why don't I leave you to get some sleep?" He lifted her arm and slipped off the bed. The lamplight cast a shadow over his lowered head, obscuring his face in darkness.

Her earlier twinge of anxiousness tightened to a knot in her stomach. "Where are you going?"

"In the other room." He twisted into his jeans and grabbed the rest of his clothes.

"Why?"

"I'm not a good sleeper. I'd keep you awake."

Shannon pulled the sheet across her body and propped herself up on one elbow. She raised an uncertain smile. "It wouldn't be so bad if you kept me awake all night."

"I have paperwork to catch up on."

Her eyes rounded. They had just shared something incredible and he *had paperwork to catch up on* as if nothing had transpired between them. The realization that she had made a huge mistake hit her full force. She couldn't believe that a man could give so much of himself and then walk away unaffected.

He bent to kiss her cheek. "Good night."

"Sure," she muttered.

He hit the light switch on his way out the door.

Once he was gone, Shannon stared into the darkness. She could still smell his musky scent on the pillow, on her body. She glanced at the door, willing him to return. When he didn't, she slid off the bed. Embarrassment mixed with rage. Apparently his idea of an adult relationship and hers were poles apart. While she hadn't expected his undying commitment, she had expected respect. She thought they had shared something special. He couldn't run away fast enough.

"You idiot," she berated herself. What made her think she could enter into a purely physical relationship? Salty tears pooled in her eyes, blurring the limited vision the hall light had afforded her.

She wriggled into her skirt and blouse. Ian was shuffling around in the living room. She had neither the strength nor the stomach to face him. The next half hour passed at an excruciatingly slow pace. She sat dead still in the ladder-back desk chair until the apartment was silent.

Grabbing her shoes in one hand and her purse in the other, she tiptoed into the hall. A low hum from the television stopped her. She peeked around the corner.

The rotten louse had no trouble sleeping on the sofa. She hoped he awakened with a neck ache. He didn't stir as she crossed the carpeted floor to the kitchen. She grabbed her underwear and shoved them in her purse then quietly padded to the front door. Even the click of the lock failed to rouse him. *Not a good sleeper?* The man was comatose.

A hollow ache pressed against her chest. He hadn't wanted to sleep with her. Why hadn't he taken her to a motel room that rented by the hour? At least she would have known what to expect.

She waited, and waited and waited for the elevator. Her gaze kept returning to the apartment door. A part of her wanted him to come after her, but he didn't. What was one more shattered illusion tonight? The elevator arrived and the hydraulic whisked her to the lobby in seconds.

The doorman gave her an odd look. She was probably a frightful sight but she was too hurt and angry to care. He hailed her a cab and discreetly asked no questions. Through her tear-filled eyes she watched the blur of neon street signs passing her by. How could a night that began with such promise end so miserably? She had a long and expensive taxi ride home to ponder the answer.

* * *

Ian bolted upright. Except for the dull hiss of the television, the apartment was silent. A pain shot through his neck as if some tribal priestess had jabbed a pin into a voodoo doll. He rubbed the sore area. As the physical pain subsided, a new and different ache seeped into his cramped muscles.

Tonight had been more than he'd bargained for. Never had he experienced such an intimate coming together. If he hadn't put some distance between himself and Shannon, he might have blurted out some sentimental words of love like an adolescent boy on a hormone rush. His body still yearned for her. Knowing she was in the other room only intensified the need.

He'd sworn he would never give a woman that kind of power over him. Yet in one passion-filled evening, Shannon had hammered a chink in the armor that surrounded his heart. How easy it would be to go back to her and let her finish the job.

Assuming she wants you back, his conscience mocked.

He should have stayed with her a while before walking out of the bedroom. Who was he kidding? He hadn't walked, he'd run.

He let out a bitter laugh. He had certainly screwed up big time. Earlier he had closed his eyes to what he hadn't wanted to see, but now he was forced to remember the wounded look in her eyes when he had pulled away. Although he hadn't intended to hurt her, only a fool would fail to know what tonight meant to her.

Shannon had lied. She wasn't the cool, detached

woman she presented to the world. Damn! This was exactly the situation he had hoped to avoid. A woman looking for a rich man to take care of her didn't warrant a thought to her feelings. A woman like Shannon, who wanted a piece of his heart, was a much greater threat to the unencumbered life-style he had perfected.

Eight

Wendy took a sip of the thick, strong brew Shannon called coffee. "I didn't expect you back so early."

Shannon wasn't up to a grilling on last night's fiasco so she gave her friend the minimum amount of information to keep Wendy's curiosity in check. "Ian has to work today."

"That never seemed to bother him before."

The shrill ring of the telephone startled Shannon. Taking a calming breath, she settled into the sofa.

"Aren't you going to answer that?" Wendy asked.

"No. The machine will pick up."

"What if it's Ian calling?"

That was precisely what worried Shannon. Three times the phone had rung but she hadn't even played back the messages. Perhaps she was being silly. Ian probably hadn't noticed her departure. Or if he had, he was no doubt thanking his lucky stars that he didn't have to deal with an awkward morning-after scene.

"Are you keeping something from me?" Wendy popped a doughnut hole into her mouth.

Shannon forced a smile. "Is it possible to keep anything from you? The *National Enquirer* calls you for information."

"You've been conspicuously tight-lipped since you put Chelsea on the bus."

She knew that only a few snippets of yesterday's details would keep her friend off her back. "That's because these lips are exhausted after last night."

"Care to elaborate?"

"Not really." Shannon faked a yawn. "I have to get some sleep. I was up all night." That wasn't a lie, even though her sleeplessness came while she was alone in her own bed.

"I can take a hint," Wendy said. "But I can't take any more of this mud you laughingly call coffee. Won't that stuff keep you awake?"

"Nothing keeps me awake."

An hour later, Shannon was still staring at the ceiling, wide awake. Her bed felt as empty as her heart. Snowball had dug himself into the pillow next to her, a constant reminder of the man who had brought the little terror into the house.

If thoughts of Ian were going to haunt her anyway, she might as well get up and put her nervous anger to some constructive work. She sat up and hit the button on her answering machine.

"Shannon. It's seven-thirty. If you had to leave early you should have told me. I would have driven you. Call me when you get in." Ian's deep voice sparked a tingling feeling in her traitorous body.

She wrapped her arms around her bent legs and rested her chin on top. The pretzel-like position didn't relieve the sensation. Reminding herself of his emotional withdrawal last night did the trick.

"Damn it. I hate these machines. It's nine o'clock. Call me when you arrive." So, he'd had a small bout of conscience when he discovered her gone. He'd get over it.

"Pick up... I know you're there... What's the idea of sneaking out in the middle of the night? When the doorman told me what time you left I had a good mind to come ring your neck. Shannon... Pick up the damn phone..." He followed with a muttered expletive and a slamming of the receiver. The anger in his voice had been unmistakable.

Rather than receive another series of calls she'd have to avoid, she dialed the business number he had given her and left a message with his secretary.

He had no right to be mad at her. She didn't owe him any explanations. They'd said their goodbyes when he had gone to sleep on the sofa. How had he walked out of the bedroom without a backward glance? Clearly she'd missed a few revealing details in her passion-fogged mind that were obvious now. He had not allowed her to touch him. The sex, although fantastic, had been distant. He had aroused her and taken her to new heights sexually but he had not granted her the pleasure of reciprocating.

She would never bridge the gulf that Ian had built around his heart. Nor would she find another man who fulfilled her erotic fantasies to such perfection. So the question she had avoided yesterday came back to haunt her today. Could she detach her emotions and deal with a purely physical relationship? She didn't know anymore.

Ian downshifted and brought the big rig to a halt in front of Shannon's ranch house. His day had gone from bad to worse. Two drivers had called in sick and one had become a father six weeks earlier than expected. Unable to find three replacements on short notice, he had had to take one of the local runs himself. Usually he enjoyed the occasional day on the open road but not today.

His company was growing faster than he'd anticipated and he needed to hire more drivers. While that might have given him a certain sense of satisfaction a couple of months ago—back then he had something to prove—now he wondered who the hell he had been trying to impress. What good was success when you had no one to share it with?

His thoughts invariably turned to Shannon and Chelsea. He raked his fingers through his hair. Just when he thought he had finally figured out the female species, Shannon went and changed the rules. She had forced a relationship with his sister on him, knowing full well he would not be able to close his heart to the bubbling three-year-old. Once the door was opened, Shannon had strolled right on in with her niece.

He swung the heavy door out and jumped down to the street. As he walked up the driveway, he noticed that Shannon's car was gone. Had she assumed he would stop by after work and made herself scarce?

"Ian." Chelsea ran across the neighbor's lawn. She tripped, picked herself up and lunged full-speed into him.

"Hey, half-pint," he said, lifting her up into the air. She squeezed a hug around his neck. He couldn't remember anyone being that excited to see him before. "Where's your aunt Shannon?"

"Her went to the store." She pointed to the metallic blue rig. "That your big truck?"

"It sure is. Do you want to go for a ride?"

Her blue eyes widened and she bobbed her head enthusiastically.

Ian started toward the truck when a terrified voice shrieked, "Put that child down." He spun back around.

Wendy came flying out of the house, her mop of curls flapping in her wake. She held a baseball bat in a vise grip, raised to strike. When she saw him, she froze for a long moment then lowered the bat to the ground with a sigh of relief. "Chelsea, honey, don't ever leave the yard without telling me first."

"Ian here."

Wendy put a hand over her chest. "I see." Three

little faces peered out from behind their shaking mother.

Ian shrugged and grinned sheepishly. "My fault. I didn't think first."

Red patches stained the woman's rounded cheeks. "Shannon didn't mention you were coming, so when my oldest son said some man was picking up Chelsea I naturally assumed...I mean, this is a safe neighborhood but..."

He waved off her apologetic explanations. "You're right. I'm sorry. Would it be all right if I took her for a ride in the truck?"

"Of course. As long as I know she's with you."

"Me, too," a chorus of young voices sang out. The two young boys and small cherub-faced girl turned pleading gazes in his direction.

Wendy mumbled, "I don't think Ian wants—"

"One kid or four makes no difference for a few turns around the block."

"If you're sure it's no trouble."

Ian eyed the Louisville Slugger in Wendy's hand and decided he would prefer his chances with four squalling children over one armed and frightened woman. "No trouble."

Shannon tucked away the last of the groceries. She had to hide the sweets from Chelsea or the child would hold off eating her other food first. Taking a minute to enjoy the solitude, she rested her arms on the kitchen counter and closed her eyes. Ian's image sprang to life in her vivid imagination.

Earlier, when Chelsea had returned from pre-school, Shannon had been able to keep her mind occupied with coloring projects and a walk to the park. Something as mundane as a trip to the super-market managed to bring Ian back into her thoughts. She found herself wondering how much food to buy. Would he have enough nerve to come spend the weekend again? Or had he caught on that she wanted to avoid him for a while?

Shannon shook her head. It was time to fetch her niece from next door and submerge herself in the mindless chatter that afforded her a modicum of distraction. She pushed off the counter and stepped out the back door.

Wendy was sitting in a lounge chair on the front lawn looking like Cleopatra on her Nile barge. "Join me."

Shannon flopped into a chair. "Where are the children?"

"They went for a ride."

"Your husband is an angel."

"My husband is working late. Ian took them."

Shannon bolted up so fast she nearly tipped the chair. "What? He took all the kids in his little sports car?"

"No. He brought his truck."

She pictured him behind the wheel of some four-wheel-drive vehicle with a macho name. "It figures he'd have more than one car."

Wendy shielded her eyes against the sun dipping in the western sky. "What's wrong with you? I thought you'd be running home to fix your makeup.''

"For him? Fat chance.''

"Did I miss something?''

Shannon sighed. "No. I did.'' Something painfully obvious. She was not the kind of woman who could drift in and out of a casual affair. "And by the way, Wendy. There is no pleasure in pure unadulterated sex. If it isn't mixed with emotions, it leaves a bitter aftertaste.''

The loud shriek of an air whistle cried in agreement. The rumbling of a large engine and the steady stream of blasting honks weren't common sounds for the quiet neighborhood. As the giant rig stopped in front of the house, Shannon saw the pack of faces pressed against the window glass. "What did he do, mug a teamster?''

When Ian had spoken of his freight company, she had envisioned him as the president of a freight forwarding firm, arranging overseas shipments for clients. Over-the-road hauling seemed too banal for his upper-class roots.

"Not the truck you expected, huh?'' Wendy asked.

"Not exactly.''

"So, maybe the man isn't what you're expecting, either. Anyone who is patient with children can't be all bad.''

Shannon didn't doubt his ability to relate to a three-year-old. It was his cynical view on adult relationships that had her worried. She reluctantly dragged herself out of the chair. "I guess I'd better start dinner."

Wendy sent her a sly wink. "The way to a man's heart?"

"More like the sooner he's fed, the sooner he'll leave."

"Right. I'll bet you five dollars that truck is still there tomorrow."

"You're on," Shannon flung over her shoulder as she sprinted across the lawn.

Three hours later, Shannon was no closer to winning her bet. Through dinner Chelsea chatted endlessly about her ride in the truck with Ian, her kitten from Ian, her brother, Ian. Ian said this. Ian did that. Shannon was waiting for him to walk on water, he was just so perfect in her niece's eyes.

Worse, he played right along with his adoring sister, shamelessly encouraging the child to pay him compliments. He knew Shannon was irritated, yet he behaved as if nothing was wrong. One big happy family sitting down to the evening meal.

Why shouldn't he enjoy the attention? He got all the benefits and security of family life with none of the responsibility.

By the time Chelsea went down for the night, Shannon was drained. Hopefully Ian would leave now that his audience was asleep. There was no one around to impress with his charm.

She had left him in the living room while she went to her own room to put laundry away. Although the wall-to-wall carpet muffled his footsteps, his musky scent alerted her to his presence in the room.

Resting his shoulder against the doorframe, he folded his arms across his chest. "Now that we're alone, clue me in as to why you felt the need to sneak out in the middle of the night."

"I didn't see any reason to stay." She closed the bureau drawer with her knee. "Clearly when the host has had enough of you, it's time to leave."

"What's that supposed to mean?"

She sat in the swivel chair at her desk. "Admit it, Ian. You weren't comfortable having me spend the night in your apartment."

His sexy half grin had her stomach doing flip-flops. "Did I seem uncomfortable?"

"Not with the sex. You were right at home in that respect. It's what happened afterward."

"Nothing happened afterward."

"Exactly."

He stepped inside and sat on the edge of her bed. The intimacy of holding a conversation in her bedroom left her off balance, but she couldn't figure out a way to leave without letting him know how his closeness rattled her.

"Did I do anything you didn't like? Because I seem to remember you were with me all the way."

Only a man would throw up something like that in an argument. "You were great. Incredible. Next time I'm in the mood for sex, I'll give you a call and book an hour of your time."

"You're being ridiculous," he said with maddening calm. "Next you'll offer to pay me."

"What's your going price?"

"Why don't you tell me what's bothering you and we'll sort it out."

Ian remained calm while she resorted to insults. She had lost control of the situation. Inhaling deeply, she drew on her inner strength. "I want a relationship, not sporadic nights of sex."

His eyes narrowed. He leaned forward and clamped his fingers over his knees. "We discussed this last night."

"We said no promises, no strings attached. But not no personal involvement. Do you realize that I know nothing about you and you only know about me what your father's sleazy detective dug up on my family?"

"What do we need to know? We're good together."

"No. You were good. I never got a chance."

He swiped at the errant lock of hair that fell across his forehead. "So…you want to be in control. Next time you can tie me to the bed and have your way with me."

"Funny joke, Ian. Anything to avoid a conversation that might require you to express emotions."

"I am not a sensitive, in-touch-with-my-feminine-side man. You knew that before we got involved. If you want to know something about me, ask. I'm not hiding anything from you."

"When I want that kind of information, I'll give you a questionnaire to fill out." With a shake of her head, she came to her feet. "It would have been nice if you had stuck around for a few minutes afterward last night and talked to me as if I were a person rather than someone you just happened to have sex with.''

"That's not what happened.'' Ian slid a hand over her hip and tugged her closer.

"It is from my perspective.'' She braced her palms against his shoulders and kept a breathable distance. Already her body began to react to his nearness. She knew just how dangerous he could be when given an inch of maneuvering room. "And I'm not ready for an encore just yet.''

"You're not being fair.''

"I think it's fair to let me build up walls first. Otherwise you'll be dealing with an emotional woman who has PMS and knows how to use a kitchen knife.''

"Okay,'' he said, releasing her slowly. "Would you like to watch television?''

"Why don't you go home?''

"Because if I did, you'd be more convinced that I'm only after sex. There's nothing more cold than a man who storms out because a woman says no to him.''

He was good. Too good. She had backed herself into a corner. He said exactly what she wanted to hear. If she insisted he leave, it was tantamount to admitting that she didn't trust herself. Which, of course, she didn't.

Nine

Ian settled himself in the chair and grinned. Sitting across from his grandfather in the office made him feel as if he had taken a step back in time. Adam looked at least ten years younger than he had only last month.

"What brings you to this neighborhood? Checking up on me?" Adam jokingly asked.

"I had to box up some things from Wesley's house before the estate sale."

Adam leaned back in the squeaky chair. "I called you last night."

"I haven't been home."

"I gathered that from the grin on your face when you entered. Someone special?"

Ian shrugged offhandedly. "Yeah."

His grandfather eyed him suspiciously. "Don't joke with an old man."

"I knew I shouldn't have said anything. You'll blow it all out of proportion."

Adam smiled sheepishly. "You can't blame me for wanting to see you settled."

"I said she was special. I didn't say I was settling down."

"It will come."

Ian chuckled. "So will another Ice Age, but hopefully not in my lifetime."

"You go right ahead and fight, boy. It will make watching you fall that much more enjoyable."

He shook his head. His grandfather would never stop trying to marry him off. Adam didn't realize that Ian's life was more settled now than it had been in the past twenty years. "How's work?" Ian asked. "Was the transition smooth?"

"No problem with the people. But this new-fangled computer system has me stymied. Voice mail, e-mail, faxes, all at the click of a button. It's a far cry from the days when I ran the show. Wesley took the company a long way."

Ian groaned. "Sure. That's because he took over an elite client base when he swindled the company from you and Mom."

Adam's eyes narrowed sorrowfully. "Let go of the past. You have a future ahead of you. Your little sister is going to need you to be there for her like I was for you."

He exhaled deeply, letting his anger recede. "Chelsea is something. She only turned three last week and already she knows how to wrap a man around her finger.''

"So, you've been seeing her.''

"Yeah.''

The admission pleased Adam. "Good for you. I have a meeting with her aunt tomorrow.''

"Why?'' Ian asked skeptically.

"It's time. She's responsible for Chelsea's finances. I need to know how she wants the money disbursed.''

"I wonder why Shannon never mentioned it.'' He didn't like her keeping things from him, but he couldn't figure out why. He had hardly been forthcoming about any area of his life.

"I only called her today. Is something wrong?'' Ian twisted his fingers together in his lap. "No.''

"So tell me about her. What's she like?''

Shannon's image came immediately to mind. "Huge brown eyes. Deep red hair with a fiery temper to match. And a pair of legs that could take your breath away.''

"In other words, she's the *someone special.*''

Ian shook his head to clear the hormone-induced stupor. "What did you say?''

"I wasn't asking for a physical description, but she seems to be indelibly etched into your mind.''

She was more than in his mind. She was under his skin, invading his blessed solitude. Last night had been torture. They'd watched television together, necking and petting like two high school teens. After the movie ended, she had made him sleep alone in the guest room.

Twelve hours later, he was still feeling the effects of his frustration. "I have to be heading back. I'll call you next week."

His grandfather's laughter mocked him. "You can't run forever."

"I can try." Despite his brave words, he was running headlong into disaster. No matter how many times, he denied the truth, even to himself, he was more involved with Shannon than was wise. He should back off before he got in any deeper, but he knew he wouldn't.

Shannon checked the address twice before entering the building. She was apprehensive about the appointment. Ian hadn't mentioned that his comptroller wanted to speak with her. In her experience, when an underling requested a private meeting, it spelled trouble. Hadn't Ian told his manager that she had no authority in running Westervelt Properties?

Perhaps she should have called Ian first. Of course, if the purpose of the meeting was aboveboard and innocent, she would be making a big deal out of nothing. She could always call him afterward.

She glanced at the name she had scrawled on the paper. Adam Westervelt. What was his connection to Westervelt Properties? Was he a one-time partner with Wesley Bradford? She wouldn't get the answer standing in the air-conditioned lobby. After checking her appearance in the glass door, she strode to the front desk.

"May I help you?" a pleasant-looking woman asked.

"I have an eleven o'clock meeting with Adam Westervelt. Shannon Moore."

"Yes, he's expecting you. Right this way." The woman led Shannon through a maze of corridors, finally pausing at a corner office. "Miss Moore is here, sir."

"Show her in," a deep voice called out cheerfully.

Shannon's first look at Adam Westervelt took her by surprise. The older man standing behind the desk was nothing like she'd expected. When they'd spoken on the phone, his baritone voice had led her to believe she'd been speaking with a younger man.

"There are some messages on your e-mail, sir," the receptionist said before closing the door behind Shannon.

Adam came around the desk and chivalrously held out a chair. "Sit down, please."

"Thank you." Shannon slipped into the leather seat with an embarrassing swoosh.

"Hate those darned chairs, myself." He gave her a fatherly smile. His clear gray eyes settled on her face, assessing her. Not in an offensive manner, but more like a man gazing at his daughter. "My grandson was right."

Shannon blinked. "Excuse me?"

Adam lowered himself into the chair behind his desk and folded his arms on top. Smile lines creased his weathered face. "Big brown eyes. Fiery red hair and...I think I'll skip the rest."

"I'm not following you, sir."

"Ian."

She swallowed hard. "You're Ian's grandfather?"

"I take it he never mentioned that he gave me his shares of the company."

Ian discuss family? He wouldn't give her the time of day unless she dragged it out of him. And even then, he'd probably be suspicious of why she wanted to know the time. "No, sir. Apparently it slipped his mind."

"That's Ian. He's a very private person."

Raising her chin slightly, she did her best not to show how his silence hurt. Did he think so little of her that he wouldn't tell her about his grandfather? "I guess that explains why your name is on the door."

"I gather he didn't tell you any of the family history."

"As you said, he's a very private person. He must have figured it was none of my business. Which I guess, technically, it isn't."

"But you're family, being the guardian of his sister. And he's fond of you."

Fond of her. That must be the old-fashioned way of saying he wanted to get her in the sack. She might have held his attention span longer than other women but Ian's feelings for her went no deeper than the physical. "Is that why you wanted to see me?"

"While I'll admit that I'm curious as to the kind of woman who would draw my grandson out of his hermit shell, I didn't realize you were the *special woman* until after I called for this meeting. I wanted to discuss Chelsea. I'm not sure how much you know about the firm or even bonds and securities.''

"I have my BA from Princeton. For the last eight years I worked for a major corporation in their investment planning division. I still retain some of my clients on a consulting basis.''

"Eight years on the inside," he muttered as if truly impressed. "You could probably teach me a thing or two.''

She smiled. "I doubt that, sir.''

"Adam," he corrected. His lips curled in the same lopsided grin Ian often adopted. "I'm surprised my grandson never mentioned your background and qualifications.''

She twisted in the seat. That Ian had mentioned her at all came as a surprise. Perhaps he was more open with his grandfather. Obviously he had a deep affection for the man to just give his half of the company to Adam. "He was more wrapped up in my family background. He's only just started to accept Chelsea as his sister.''

"He's slow to come around, but once he does…''

"Don't misunderstand me. He's very good to Chelsea. She thinks the sun rises and sets on his say-so.'' Isn't that what she had asked of him? The deal was that he maintain a relationship with Chelsea, not her. "As I told Ian, I don't plan to make a nuisance of myself regarding Westervelt Properties. Whatever you decide is fine.''

Adam rubbed a finger over his bushy brow. "You must have some idea how you'd like Chelsea's money invested."

"Long term. I don't need it. T-bills and an equity fund. Perhaps you might risk a small amount in a Magellan Fund."

"Stocks?"

"Maybe later, if the money is there."

Adam grinned. "If this company keeps growing as it has in the past few years, you'll be making that decision sooner rather than later."

"I'm sure you'll keep things running smoothly or Ian wouldn't have given you the helm."

His eyes narrowed. "Yes, he would have, but I'd rather let him explain why."

On that cryptic note, Shannon came to her feet. She had a feeling that Ian's family history would read like a sweeping saga filled with deceit, betrayal and corporate intrigue. Unfortunately, she couldn't see a happily-ever-after because too many chapters of his life were missing.

"I have to meet a client in New York this afternoon. It was a pleasure meeting you, Adam."

"Likewise." He rose and pulled a brightly wrapped package from his desk drawer. "For the little birthday girl."

For several awkward seconds she stared at the box. Her own parents hadn't remembered let alone acknowledged their granddaughter's birthday. "Thank you."

"My pleasure." Adam placed a hand on her

shoulder as he walked her to the door. "And don't give up."

The way he smiled led her to believe he had a hidden agenda. Not with malicious intent, but a misguided notion of playing matchmaker. While she would gladly accept any help in breaking through the granite wall that surrounded Ian's emotions, she knew it would take more than the good-hearted overtures of the old man.

Shannon strode down Wall Street at a brisk pace. With luck she could get to the train station and out to the park-n-ride before the heaviest of the rush-hour commuters left work for the weekend. Weaving through the slower pedestrians, she headed for the bus stop.

Her feet began to feel the pinch of her high heels. If she chose, she could be at Ian's apartment in less than fifteen minutes. The idea was tempting. All she would have to do is swallow her pride and accept that he wasn't capable of giving any more of himself. After weighing the cost, she discarded the plan. She wasn't ready to give up yet.

She paused at the corner to wait for the traffic light to change. Yellow cabs and cars sped along the street, leaving a choking stream of carbon monoxide in the humid air. A limousine took the corner too fast, coming dangerously close to the curb. She jumped backward, bumping into a solid frame.

"Excuse me," she mumbled as she tried to inch away. Something seemed to be tugging at her, preventing her withdrawal.

For a split second her heart seemed to stop. Her body went rigid. She stiffened her arm, pinning her handbag against her waist.

Without thinking she whirled around, coming face-to-face with a toothless, mangy-haired man. A clicking sound drew her attention to his switch-blade, glinting silver in the afternoon sun. Instinctively, she locked a vise grip on her purse.

"Hand it over." His voice was a menacing rumble of rage.

Her mind refused to cooperate with her body and she struggled.

"Stupid witch," he snarled. In a flash, he cut at the leather strap, slicing the razor-sharp blade into her arm, as well. Her purse was yanked free. As the man shoved past her to make his escape, she stumbled into a car that had stopped for the light.

Pain shot though her. She brought her hand up to cover the gash. Blood poured from the wound, covering the pale blue sleeve that had been shredded. Someone screamed, thankfully, since nothing came out of Shannon's open mouth.

"Did you see that?"

"Are you all right, miss?"

"She needs an ambulance."

"Someone call the police."

The words of the curious onlookers jumbled together in her head. Someone helped her from the street to the sidewalk. She leaned against a light post. Her thoughts remained scattered. She could neither think nor answer the questions directed at her, only stare after the assailant who had long since disappeared into the city streets.

Ian sprinted down the corridor to the emergency room desk. A waiting room full of patients moaned and groaned, adding to his anxiety. As he waited through the short line of people in front of him, he tapped his keys against the counter. Several people glared at him and he stopped.

"May I help you?" the receptionist finally asked.

"I'm here to pick up a patient who was brought in earlier. Shannon Moore."

The plump woman checked the computer. "Room four."

Ian nodded his thanks and elbowed his way through the door. Although brightly lit, the bustling halls seemed darkly imposing.

The last time he had been to a hospital had been when his mother died. The memories were more than he cared to deal with in his present frame of mind.

When he entered room number four, he found Shannon sitting on the end of a gurney, her legs dangling over the edge. Her right arm was bandaged and several surface scratches marred her pale complexion. A uniformed police officer stood at the side of the bed taking notes. She snapped her pad closed and sent Shannon a reassuring smile.

"I think your ride is here."

Shannon glanced up. "Ian!" Her voice broke and she cleared her throat before continuing. "What are you doing here?"

"Wendy called me. She couldn't get a sitter. Are you all right?"

"Yeah."

The officer touched her shoulder. "She's a fighter. That's what landed her here to begin with. She didn't want to give up her purse."

"It was a reaction, not bravery," Shannon said.

"And damned stupid," Ian growled. He knew his anger was misdirected, but seeing her battered and bandaged body filled him with a host of emotions he didn't know how to deal with.

Shannon rolled her eyes. "May I leave?"

"I'm finished for now," the policewoman said. "If we turn up anything we'll give you a call."

Ian stepped aside to let the officer leave. When he turned back he noticed Shannon had jumped from the gurney and walked to the chair to get her clothes. Her skirt hadn't fared badly, but her blouse was a loss.

Removing his own shirt, he slipped it around Shannon's shoulders. "Why didn't you call me?"

She gingerly pushed her arms through the sleeves. "Do we have to get into it here?"

Her distance and self-control made him even madder. Didn't she realize how seriously she could have been hurt?

"No. We'll discuss it back at the apartment." He fastened the buttons, keeping her close to him as he worked his fingers down the shirt. The aroma of antiseptic mingled with her perfume. "Where's your car?"

"At a park-n-ride," she said. "You can drop me off there."

"I'll take you there tomorrow."

"Chelsea..." Worry for the child brought the first flicker of emotion to her face.

"Is spending the night with your friend. She'll be fine. Are we in agreement now?"

She turned her palms upward in a gesture of defeat. "Since I don't have any money, I haven't got a lot of choices on the subject."

"I'm glad you see it my way."

After Shannon signed the release form, they left the hospital. Cupping his hand over her elbow, he led her to the parking garage across the street. He noticed the way she cringed when the garage attendant walked toward them with a wide grin. They did make an odd pair. He, in his dress slacks and T-shirt and Shannon in a gray linen skirt and his Oxford shirt.

Once his car was brought around, Ian settled Shannon in the passenger seat before paying the attendant and pulling out into the evening traffic.

He glanced over at her. She sat ramrod straight in the bucket seat with her fingers locked around the handgrip and her eyes squeezed shut. Apparently, she was unimpressed by his impeccable driving record. He wasn't sure if it was a delayed reaction to her ordeal or a clever ruse to avoid talking to him. Whichever, he decided to wait until he got her home to question her.

Ten

Ian returned from the kitchen with a glass of water. In the ten minutes they'd been in the apartment, Shannon hadn't said one word about the incident that had landed her in the hospital. She made a quick call to Wendy to let her friend know she wouldn't be home for the night, then launched into a rambling speech about the stark decor of his home. As if he gave a damn about decorating in the best of circumstances.

He handed her the glass.

"Thanks," she said. "You know, a couple of brightly colored pillows would really liven up the place."

Unable to bare the inane small talk for one more minute he grumbled, "Damn it, Shannon, didn't anyone ever tell you not to fight with a mugger?"

She exhaled a sigh. "Of course."

"You're not wise enough to be left on your own in the city. What were you doing here anyway? I thought you had a meeting with my grandfather today."

Her eyes widened in surprise. "He told you?"

Ian nodded.

She took a sip of water an put the glass on the table. "I had some business to take care of afterward."

"That's the second time this week," he noted. "What kind of business is so important that you had to risk your safety?"

She let out an exasperated groan. "Forget it." As she sprang to her feet, he caught her around the waist. She twisted against him. "I'm going home. I'll send the shirt back to you after I have it cleaned."

"You're not going anywhere. You don't have any money."

"I'll walk. It's better than staying here while you tell me how I deserved to be mugged, in broad daylight, down in the financial district. Which, I might point out, is one of the safer areas of the city."

He *was* blaming her. How juvenile could he get? "Fine. You're right. I'm wrong."

She stopped her squirming and glanced up at him. "What's the punch line?"

"Why didn't you call me?"

"Why would I?"

"I thought we were…uh…"

"Involved? Committed? In a relationship? Precisely which one of those words is making you choke?" Her stinging barbs landed with lethal accuracy. Without a struggle from him, she stepped out of his embrace. "I was going to call you, but then, I didn't want to bother you."

"Bother me? Give me some credit."

"Isn't this what you wanted to avoid? A silly woman who bothers you for every little thing."

"Call me because you break a fingernail and I'll get ticked off. I think you can safely assume that I'd want to know if you were in the hospital."

"I wasn't even admitted. It was a couple of stitches."

"Twelve is not a couple."

Shannon sighed. "Remind me to shoot Wendy when I see her again. She shouldn't have called you."

"If she hadn't, you'd still be sitting in the hospital."

"At least the nurses didn't treat me like a child," she complained.

"I know you better."

"If we're gong to fight all night, I'm leaving."

Even though he knew he should back off, he couldn't. The fact that she hadn't called him was a source of irritation. "Do you want Chelsea to see you looking like this?"

She shook her head. "No. But I can't avoid her until all the cuts and bruises heal."

"True, but tomorrow you'll be less frightened."

"I'm not frightened. I'm mad. The lousy bastard got all my credit cards and money, not to mention my keys. And the locksmith won't change the locks until I'm there.''

"I'll do it tomorrow. Why don't I go out to get us something to eat?"

"No!" She clasped her hand over his arm. "I'm not very hungry."

Obviously, she didn't want him to leave. So, Shannon was not as in control as she'd like him to believe. She needed him. Normally that was enough to send him running from a relationship. Only, he had no desire to flee. If anything, he felt relieved. "All right. You can take a bath while I make a couple of sandwiches."

Shannon lowered herself into the hot water with a sigh. Resting her bandaged arm on the edge of the porcelain tub, she let the warmth ease the tension from her tired limbs. Memories of the day's events wouldn't allow her to fully unwind. She had lived in the city for years without incident. If she had kept alert instead of thinking about Ian, she might not have made such a perfect victim.

She closed her eyes and enjoyed the silence. One more lecture from Ian and she would scream. The emergency room nurse had warned her that he might have this kind of reaction. Since he'd been powerless to protect her, he would lash out.

A soft knock broke her peaceful bliss. "Are you decent?" he called.

She slipped deeper into the water. "No."

"Good." He walked into the bathroom, holding

a mobile phone. "Chelsea wants to speak with you."

"How much did you tell her?"

"Nothing. She thinks we're having a pajama party. I could hardly tell her that our sleepovers don't involve pajamas."

She crinkled her nose and took the receiver from him. "Hi, Chels. What are you doing?... Simba again?... Are you being good for Wendy?... Yes, Ian is coming tomorrow... A present, too? We'll see, if you're a good girl for Wendy... I love you, too... 'Bye, bye... No, you hang up first." When she heard the click she hit the disconnect button and put the phone on the floor.

Ian sat on the edge of the tub and pushed a damp strand of hair off her cheek. His gaze wandered over her body but his expression remained impassive.

"You're staring," she said.

"Just thinking about physics."

"Nuclear or astro?"

"Neither. The properties of buoyancy."

She glanced down and saw the pink tips of her breasts bobbing in the water. Refusing to let him throw her off balance, she shrugged. "At my age, I'll take all the help I can get."

His rich laughter sounded good, as if his earlier anger had dissipated. "Do you want me to wash your back?"

"No, thanks."

His finger trailed from her cheek to her shoulder,

drawing sweeping circular patterns over her wet skin. "How about your front?"

She splashed a handful of water at him. "Cool off."

"Impossible."

"Be careful, Ian, or I might mistake you for someone who cares."

"Why would you think I didn't."

Her jaw dropped open slightly. "Maybe because you go to such extraordinary lengths to suppress your feelings."

"At least I'm consistent."

"Consistently infuriating," she agreed. "Could you pass me a towel?"

"Are you finished?"

She shook her head. "It's not relaxing anymore."

"I didn't mean to distract you."

"Then take your hand off my breast."

His thumb ran one more seductive stroke over the taut nipple before he slipped his hand around to her back and hauled her out of the tub with ease. She dripped water over his T-shirt and jeans as he folded his arms around her trembling body. A towel might have been more effective for drying her, but for sheer warmth, his embrace won hands down.

The gentle pressure of his lips against her temple sent a new and infinitely more pleasurable tremor through her. She tipped her head up. He gave her a chaste kiss and turned her loose.

Before she had time to protest or even notice the cool rush of air, he had removed a bathrobe off a peg on the door and pulled it around her. The bulky garment engulfed her body in plush terry cloth. The sleeves hung six inches beyond her fingertips.

Ian ran his gaze along the length of her, covered from neck to toes. "There. Now, maybe I can behave myself."

She stomped her foot. "Well, who asked you to?"

His eyes sparkled with humor. "What, no tirade on my arrogant, conceited and cold personality? Obviously, you're still disoriented. You need to have a bite to eat, maybe call your mother..."

"What on earth for?"

He slipped his arm across her back and led her to the living room. "Don't women usually call their mothers when they've been through an ordeal?"

"Not unless I want the added guilt of giving her an anxiety attack. She tends to make herself the center of any crisis whether she is involved or not."

He arched an eyebrow. "Your father?"

"He wouldn't be interested unless he could find a way to blame my mother." She sat on the sofa, folding her legs to the side. "Tiffany would have listened. Then she would have told me I was a jackass for not kicking the creep where it counted."

The mental image caused Ian to groan. "Your sister had a charming manner."

"What she lacked in tact she made up for in sheer tenacity. She knew what she wanted and she went after it. In different circumstances you probably would have admired her determination, if not her methods."

Memories of Tiffany hit Shannon hard. She'd never had time to grieve the loss of her sister because the early days with Chelsea had been so difficult.

Ian gazed down at her curiously. "You loved your sister?"

She brushed away a solitary tear. "Of course. Does that surprise you? I might not have agreed with the way she conducted her life, but she was my family."

Ian settled into the corner of the sofa. "Family ties only count for so much."

"You must think they count for something. You gave Adam your half of Wesley's company."

"It was never Wesley's company. I just returned a property to its rightful owner."

"Then how did your father get control?"

He paused for a long moment. Thinking about the past churned-up years of resentment. He didn't want conflicting emotions distorting his perception tonight.

But Shannon was waiting for an answer. Although he had been successful at keeping her at a distance, she had made it clear she wouldn't accept his evasions much longer.

"When my mother was in the hospital battling breast cancer, he used the power of attorney she'd signed to transfer her shares into his name. Coupled with the twenty percent of the company Adam gave him when he married my mother, he had controlling interest."

Ian clenched and unclenched his fingers, his stan-

dard reaction whenever he talked about his es-
tranged father. "Two years afterward, when he was
firmly in power, Wesley divorced my mother. She
didn't even try to take him to court to get the company back. She took her settlement in cash and
bowed out."

Until now, Ian had never realized how much his
mother's capitulation had clouded his views of
women. He had seen her strength in her ardent fight
with cancer, yet in terms of her husband, she had
always been weak. The years of lies and infidelity
she had put up with rather than give up her way of
life. Even in the end, she went for the money rather
than the fight.

"Adam still had a piece of the company."

"Taking a back seat in the company he'd
founded was intolerable. He sold out to Wesley and
took early retirement."

Shannon lowered her head onto Ian's shoulder.
"Too bad. Your grandfather is such a nice man."

Ian shrugged. "Yeah, he's great. It's probably his
biggest character flaw."

"How so?"

"He trusts too easily and ends up burned. At one
time he admired Wesley, respected his drive and
ambition. Look where that got him."

"That's your father's character flaw, not
Adam's."

"You can't run a successful business by being a
nice guy."

She tipped her head up to meet his gaze. "Maybe

family was more important to him than a successful business.''

''In the end, he lost both.''

''He still has you.''

He let out a bitter laugh. ''And isn't that a prize for him?''

''I don't know. You have your moments.'' She ran her hand along his muscular thigh, eliciting a deep groan from him. ''Too bad they're so few and far between.''

Clasping his fingers over her wrist, he stopped her wayward hand. ''Don't start with me, Shannon.''

''Are you going to wuss out on me?''

This time his laughter was rich and genuine. She had an uncanny ability to get him talking, but more importantly, she knew when to back off. ''I know teamsters who talk nicer than you.''

''Yeah, I know. And I've improved since I got custody of Chelsea. I'm sorry I'm not like the socialites you're used to.''

He pulled her into his lap, cuddling her against him. ''How would you know what I'm used to?''

''You don't trust women whose bank accounts are lower than yours.''

''I don't trust women who want to be kept in the style their daddies made them accustomed to, either.''

''You don't like the rich ones, you don't like the poor ones. You're closing a lot of doors. What are you leaving yourself with?''

''You.''

For how long? she almost asked, but she didn't want to know the answer. Not tonight. She needed his closeness, his strength. At the same time, she despised her weakness and vulnerability. She needed to feel in control again.

"You're not going to argue? You must be ill. I'll put you to bed."

She smiled up at him. "Sounds good."

"Alone," he amended.

Her hand came out from beneath the floppy sleeve to gently smack his shoulder. "No food. No sex. I'm never coming back to this joint again."

"For a woman who didn't want to call me today, you're awfully anxious for my company."

Despite the teasing tone in his voice, Shannon read the underlying accusation. "Are we back to that again?"

"I don't want you to think you can't call me. I care about you and Chelsea and I want you to call if there's a problem."

His words were spoken with such sincerity that she dared to hope that he might be coming around. "Okay. The next time I get mugged I'll give you a jingle."

Anger flared in his blue eyes but quickly receded when he caught her grin. With an exasperated groan, he said, "Let me get your sandwich."

"I'd rather eat afterward."

"After what?"

She slipped her fingers under his still-damp T-shirt. "After I build up an appetite." At her playful probing his stomach muscles bunched.

"You have twelve stitches on your arm and assorted bruises and cuts."

Her spirits sank. "I guess I don't look very appealing right now."

He exhaled deeply. "That's the trouble. You're too damned appealing. I'd be so conscious about hurting you that I'd probably end up hurting you."

"Then I'll just have to take charge this time." She unbuckled his belt and tugged open the zipper of his jeans. Slipping her hand inside, she closed her fingers around his hard shaft. "You can handle that, can't you?"

Ian sucked in a large gulp of air. "Probably not."

"Even better." She stroked him repeatedly.

His breathing became shallow and his eyes glazed over. "You keep doing that and it will be over before we've begun."

Shannon smiled. The emotional payoff of seeing him lose his strict self-control and give in to his desires would be worth as much as a satisfying physical conclusion.

After pulling his shirt over his head, she worked her way down his broad shoulders and chest with her tongue, drinking in the woodsy scent of him.

Tenderly, he traced a line around the bandage on her arm. "Are you sure?"

She nodded.

Although Ian seemed less than convinced, he rose to his feet, lowering her to the floor. He stripped off his jeans and tossed them aside. When he reached for Shannon, she pushed him back onto the sofa and straddled herself across his legs. The bulky white robe slipped from her shoulders.

"Make sure you tell me if I hurt you," he said.

He took one breast into his calloused hand and rolled the pebbled tip between his thumb and forefinger. Her sigh of pleasure was silenced beneath the pressure of his mouth on hers. He traced her lips with his tongue, then plundered inside, filling her with the heated taste of him.

Her heart beat a little faster. Anticipation mounted.

"Wouldn't you be more comfortable in the bedroom?" he muttered.

"No." She wriggled forward, opening her thighs wider at the pressure of his full arousal. Raising to her knees, she used her trembling hand to guide him inside her.

A breath caught in her throat. Oh, he felt good! She twisted against him until he filled her completely.

Ian's expression was one of near pain. "This isn't going to work." He tried to tip her onto her back.

She locked her fingers behind his head and began a rocking motion. "This will work fine." A power struggle had begun; one she had no intention of losing.

He clamped his palms on her hips, forcing a slow, sensual rhythm when she would have hurried the pace. "Easy."

"Not this time," she whispered.

Despite his determined efforts to take charge,

Ian's control continued to slip away. She arched in closer, clenching her muscles against each of his thrusts. His deep groan reverberated in the ear he was nibbling on.

This is what I need, she thought. There were no calculated moves or restrained reactions. Just his body responding to the pleasure of being joined with hers.

Ian's rhythm became faster, harder. The sensations stirring inside her begged for release, but she did nothing to prolong the inevitable. She caught his lower lip between her teeth and sucked on the flesh.

His climax came fast but she felt no disappointment. Partly because she knew his pride would spur him to get even later. But mostly, she wanted him to trust her enough to let down his defenses. And he did. However, if his narrowed eyes and squared jaw were any indication, he didn't enjoy abdicating power even for a while.

"I'm sorry." He forced out his apology without a trace of sincerity.

"I'm not." She ran her fingers through his silky hair. "You'll get me later."

"You're damn right I will," he vowed as if it were a matter of honor. His unsteady breathing against her neck sent erotic chills along her spine.

"Oh, put your male ego aside and tell me with all honesty that you didn't enjoy having me make love to you for a change."

He opened his mouth, then snapped it shut again.

He'd never admit the truth, but at least he didn't lie. His silence was all the proof she needed. Perhaps Ian was finally learning how to share control instead of grasping at it like a lifeline.

Eleven

Ian stared at Shannon as she played with the hair on his chest. Of course he enjoyed having her make love to him. On a purely physical level, he couldn't exactly fake it, but he didn't like losing the advantage. In his relationships, as with his business, he avoided debts. Lately he'd been taking more from Shannon than he'd been giving.

"Are you hungry now?" he asked.

Her saucy grin mocked him. She twisted purposefully in his lap. "Are you?"

"No, damn it, but I had my fill. You didn't."

She laughed and pressed her forehead against his. "What a macho idiot you are. Tonight wasn't about sex."

"Good thing," he grumbled.

"Sometimes you are so dense. I got what I needed. I think you got something nice, too."

He lowered his head onto her shoulder and nipped at the satiny skin. This woman who accepted little and gave so much was surely driving him insane. She didn't react the way he expected. To his surprise, he felt slighted that she chose to deal with her fears alone rather than lean on him. Hadn't he made the rules? *Nothing heavy or serious. No strings attached.*

He needed to get himself back on an equal footing before she realized how much power she had over his body as well as his heart. "Hightail it to the bedroom. I'll bring your sandwich."

"Dinner in bed. You spoil me."

"Don't get used to it," he jokingly warned.

"I wouldn't dream of it."

As she slid off him, a cool chill replaced the warmth she had provided. Odd, he thought, since the temperature wasn't particularly cold in the apartment. She grabbed the robe from the floor and padded across the carpet to the bedroom.

After pulling on his jeans, he went to get the sandwiches he had made earlier and joined Shannon. She had put on his T-shirt and slipped under the black-and-white bedspread. Although she smiled at him, she didn't look relaxed in her surroundings. Was her ordeal finally beginning to sink in or was something else bothering her?

"I want to get home early. Chelsea might start to think she's been abandoned again. I try not to stay away from her for too long."

He sat on the end of the bed, facing Shannon. "I guess it's hard to make a three-year-old understand things happen that can't be helped."

"It frightens her. Routine is comforting to a child."

"And to you?"

She took a bite of her sandwich. A spark of sadness caused her eyes to shimmer like liquid gold. "Sometimes it's better not to get used to things. Especially when someone else can take it away. It gives that person too much power over you. But then, I suspect you already know that." Shannon shrugged and finished her sandwich.

Her philosophy paralleled his own. So, having found a woman who understood him perfectly, why did he have the urge to change her mind? Was he so hypocritical that he needed to have a hold over her while still maintaining a comfortable emotional distance himself? Or had he done the incredibly stupid—fallen in love with her? The thought was too frightening to consider tonight.

"Do you want something to drink?"

She shook her head.

"Sleep?"

"Not if I'm going to be alone. I'll just sit here until we leave in the morning."

"Shannon…" Did she realize what she was asking?

"No one's forcing you to stay. Go sleep in front of the television. I'll read." She swiped a book from the table.

"That's an owner's manual for a Mac truck."

"It's fascinating," she said, thumbing through the pages. "By tomorrow I'll be an expert. I might even join the flipping teamsters."

"With that mouth of yours, you'll fit right in." Ian took the plates from the bed and put them on the dresser. "If I stay, you're going to sleep."

"Oh, don't worry. Your virtue is safe for the rest of the night."

His peace of mind, on the other hand, was in serious trouble. He couldn't leave, and staying would plunge him further into a situation he had spent a lifetime trying to avoid. As a compromise, he decided to stay until she fell asleep. He reached for the blanket.

"Take your pants off," she ordered.

With a shake of his head, he stripped off his jeans and climbed into the bed. She smiled and he would have sworn her eyes were sparkling triumphantly. His nagging feeling of doubt was obliterated as she curled her body around his. Her skin felt like cool satin. If he wasn't careful, he could get used to this.

He stroked her hair, her shoulder, the small indentation of her waist. She sighed and snuggled closer. After a few minutes, her breathing slowed and fell into a regular pattern. He closed his eyes and inhaled the sweet scent of her.

The physical benefits aside, he was amazed by how much he enjoyed holding her. The intimacy of sleeping together aroused emotions of a possessive nature. Emotions he'd just as soon not feel. As if he had any choice in the matter.

"I love you."

Her barely whispered words sent a screaming jolt through him. His heart thumped against his chest. Perhaps she was talking in her sleep. He remained utterly still, pretending to be asleep himself.

"Ian?"

Now he was stuck. If he answered, she would know he was awake. He couldn't claim he hadn't heard her declaration. But he'd vowed never to speak those words to any woman and he wasn't ready to break that vow. Even for Shannon.

So much for leaving once she fell asleep. He had to stay or admit to being a liar as well as a coward. Resigned to spending the night wide awake, he was more than a little surprised when he found himself drifting off into a peaceful and heavy slumber.

Shannon knew the second Ian had fallen asleep and it had been long after she'd admitted her love for him. His silence hurt, but it came as no surprise. At least he hadn't bolted from the bed.

Exhaling a wistful sigh, she nuzzled in closer for what might be her last night with Ian. What possessed her to say something so stupid? She knew he wanted to avoid emotional encumbrances. *No strings attached.*

Either he would discover she was offering him the ties that bind or figure she had presented him with a noose. She couldn't change his opinion any more than she could have held in the words. Didn't he realize she was just as frightened of losing herself as he was? Would he care if he knew?

* * *

Shannon grabbed the package from the back seat of the car and stepped onto the driveway. Ian's truck, parked by the curb, loomed like a blue giant on the narrow street. He had taken his rig to deliver the several boxes from his father's house that now cluttered her porch.

After breakfast he had taken her to the park-n-ride for her car. Thankfully, she had a spare key wired to her bumper, courtesy of the only useful advice her father had ever given her. Ian had followed her as far as the highway, then left her in the wake of his powerful machine.

She rested against one of the large cartons on the porch, wondering how to get in without keys when the front door swung open wide. A breath caught in her throat and she jumped back.

Ian stepped outside. "I didn't mean to scare you."

"How…did you get…in?" she stammered, her heart still pounding against her ribs.

"The kitchen window. You really should lock it when you go away overnight."

She inhaled deeply to calm herself. "I thought you went next door to get Chelsea."

"I'm going now. Although, you might want to get changed before she sees you."

"Why?" she asked, glancing at the oversize sweatshirt that covered her linen skirt. "Do I look that bad?"

"I didn't mean to imply…"

"That I look like something Snowball dragged in?"

He shrugged. "I think I better go before I end up in trouble."

"We need to talk, Ian."

"Later. Chelsea is waiting." He jumped from the top step and crossed the lawn as if the devil was at his heels.

Later. As if they could have a serious conversation about their relationship with a child demanding their constant attention. Did he plan to put her off indefinitely? What would he do if she pushed the issue?

She should have cornered him this morning. He had been talkative, although he'd made no mention of her declaration of love and she had been too afraid to bring it up. At the hospital yesterday she had refused to let herself be ruled by fear. Why did the thought of a conversation with Ian leave her feeling more vulnerable than her ordeal with a mugger? Possibly because she had so much more to lose than her purse.

Sidestepping the boxes, she walked into the house. Snowball let out a tiny meow and scampered across the carpet to meet her. She bent to scoop up the kitten before he tried to claw his way up her again.

"You must be hungry."

Snowball nuzzled against her neck and purred as she scratched the fur behind his ear. When she stopped, the animal squirmed to be freed.

"Typical male," she moaned as she put him on the floor again. "You want to be fed. You want to be petted, but the minute I try to hold you, you run for the nearest hiding place.''

Ian settled himself into the chair with a beer and watched while Chelsea and Shannon sat at the coffee table coloring pictures. He couldn't say that Shannon had much more talent than his sister but she had a tremendous amount of patience, even when Chelsea had tried to draw a picture on Shannon's bandaged arm.

"For Ian," Chelsea declared and lifted a paper from the table. She climbed into his lap and offered him the masterpiece of colored lines.

"Thank you."

She threw her arms around his neck. "I love you."

"I love you, too, squirt." His words tumbled out without thought. He caught the pained expression in Shannon's face before she turned away to clear the table.

His stomach knotted. She knew he had heard her declaration last night, knew he had consciously chosen to say nothing. Still, he couldn't find the words.

"Oh, Chelsea, I have something for you." Shannon disappeared into the kitchen and returned with a box. She sat on the sofa and helped the child with the wrapping paper. "This is from Ian's grandfather."

Surprised, Ian leaned forward in the chair to peek into the box. The antique doll was one he recognized well. Adam had bought the Madame Alexander doll when his daughter had been born. Ian's mother had saved it for the day he would have a daughter of his own.

"You have to be careful with that, peanut. She'll break." Shannon's gaze locked on his. "Is something wrong?"

"No."

Chelsea danced around the room, cuddling the gift as if it were a baby. Although he had a great affection for the child, she was his sister, not his daughter. In fact, she was Wesley's daughter. A by-product of one of his many affairs.

"Obviously, something is wrong," Shannon said, breaking into his thoughts. "If that's a family heirloom, save it. I can get her something else."

"I said nothing's wrong. My grandfather wanted her to have it. That's good enough for me."

Adam's gift was as much a message to Ian as a token to Chelsea. It was a message he wasn't ready to receive. Pressure came at him from all sides. He would not be badgered.

He came to his feet. "I have to go out for a while."

Shannon fidgeted with the hem of her shorts and avoided his gaze. "Will you be back for dinner?"

"Probably not."

"I come, too, Ian?" Chelsea asked.

He ruffled her silky hair. "Not this time, squirt."

A tiny hand tugged at his shirt. "I go with you?"

"No, Chelsea."

Shimmering tears streamed down her cheeks. "I can go, too, Aunt Shane?"

Shannon shook her head. "Another time. We promised to visit with Anna and Wendy. Go put your doll away first."

The alternate plan seemed to appease the child but the sad-eyed look didn't leave her face as she turned and walked away.

Ian nodded a grateful thanks. "I appreciate it."

"Sure. Anything to make it easier on you. Go on. Go. Before she tries to change your mind again."

He hesitated. Damn! She knew how to make him feel guilty. "I'll be back later."

She shrugged and grabbed the crayons off the table. He knew he should say something, but before he could speak, she had left him standing alone in the living room.

Confusion was not an emotion he handled well. He shoved his hands into his pockets for his keys, spun around and walked to the door. After checking the lock, he made his way to the truck. A few hours of solitude should clear his troubling thoughts.

Shannon stared into the darkness, unable to sleep despite her exhaustion. Nearly an hour had passed since she had gone to her room and she was no closer to drifting off now than when she had flopped down on the bed. She heard the rumble of Ian's truck and the slam of the big rig's door. Ten o'clock. Was this his idea of returning later? For the better part of the evening she'd had to explain his absence to Chelsea, who asked for him continuously. She should have locked him out instead of leaving the house unlocked in anticipation of his return.

The clatter of his keys hitting a table echoed through the silent house. She listened for footsteps heading toward the bedroom but heard nothing. Any hope that he wanted to talk with her faded quickly. If he expected her to go to him, he was in for a long, cold night.

The sounds of rattling and tapping came first from the kitchen and then the living room. She buried her head under the pillow and tried to block out the noise. Thankfully, Chelsea was a heavy sleeper. What the heck was he doing at this hour of the night? Her curiosity got the better of her determination to ignore him. She slipped from the bed and quietly made her way down the hall.

The front door was wide open, braced between Ian's knees. The porch lights bathed him in a bright glow. He was changing the door lock, just as he had promised he would. Any normal man would have waited until morning. But then, she had known from the beginning, Ian wasn't any normal man.

He turned his blue eyes toward her and shrugged an apology. "I didn't mean to wake you."

Shannon folded her arms across her chest and tapped her foot impatiently against the floor. "Yes, you did."

"I did?"

"Yeah. You wanted me to see you doing something nice so I wouldn't be angry anymore."

He arched his eyebrow. "Did it work?"

Yes, damn you, it did. And it irritated her that he knew her so well.

"Jackass," she muttered, and spun around.

"It really turns me on when you curse at me," he called after her.

"Then you would have had an orgy earlier."

Ian watched her storm down the hall, her long bare legs moving with a graceful stride. Once again he had stalled a confrontation, but for how long?

He collected his tools and returned them to the toolbox. Tomorrow he would take care of the back door and she wouldn't have to worry that the mugger had made off with her house keys. For now, he had a sultry redhead with a fiery temper to take care of.

The bedroom door was slightly ajar. He stepped inside. A sliver of moonlight illuminated the four-poster bed, where Shannon had stretched out on top of the comforter. Auburn hair fell across the pillow like a halo framing an angelic face.

She didn't comment as he shed his clothes. Nor did she take her eyes off him. It's too easy, he thought. He was surely walking into an ambush.

"You know, you're free to go sleep in the guest room," she said.

"Is that what you want?"

"No."

Honest, simple and to the point. He lay down next to her. "Then what do you want?"

Shannon turned on her side and propped her head up with one hand. "I don't want anything. Haven't you figured that out yet?"

"You don't expect me to spill my guts out like a hormone-rushed adolescent?"

She expelled a sigh. "I'd rather you say nothing than have you tell me a pack of lies."

"I am more involved than I've ever been with anyone." He slipped his leg in between hers and fitted her under his hip. "I need time to get used to the idea."

"Time you have, Ian." She cuddled against him and splayed her fingers across his back. "But if you expect me to keep my feelings bottled up until you feel comfortable, I can't do that."

He stroked a finger along her arm, gently running the perimeter of the gauze bandage. "I'm not asking you to."

With a long, deep kiss, he cut off any reply. At least he knew how to distract her. Because in truth, he would prefer she kept her feelings to herself until he knew how to deal with them. And he knew with certainty, whether consciously or subconsciously, he would probably do everything in his power to make sure she did just that.

Twelve

Shannon glanced around the restaurant that graced the lobby of the four-star hotel. She had attended more business lunches than she could count but today she had a hard time keeping her mind on business. All through the meal, her mind kept wandering to Ian. Although their weekend had ended better than it had begun, there were still many issues unresolved. She had asked him to meet her after work today to clear the air.

A discreet cough brought her back to the meeting at hand. Her client, Arthur Merring, was a sweet gentleman, a throwback to the 1950's. He had been her first client when she had begun working. Despite her move to corporate accounts, she continued to serve him. They had concluded their business earlier but he'd insisted on waiting with Shannon until her "date" arrived to pick her up. Apparently the midwestern retailer had seen one too many movies about the big, bad city. After her experience last week, she didn't argue.

She glanced at her watch. "You really don't have to wait any longer, Mr. Merring. He'll be here any minute."

"Arthur," he corrected. "And I don't mind. I'm just staying in a room upstairs. What kind of man would leave a lady by herself in the city?"

The average New Yorker, Shannon thought.

After five more minutes of polite small talk, she finally saw Ian across the room. She raised her hand to get his attention and smiled as he came up next to her.

He glanced at Mr. Merring then back to her. "Sorry I'm late." His words were friendly, but his eyes held a spark of anger.

Shannon placed a lingering hand on his arm. "Arthur Merring, this is Ian Bradford."

Arthur stood and offered his hand. "A pleasure."

"Likewise," Ian muttered.

After a long, awkward pause, Arthur cleared his throat. "Well, I'll be going. I'll see you next time I'm in town, Shannon."

She nodded and waited until he disappeared before turning to Ian. "Do you want to stay?"

He shook his head. "Where's the check?"

"It's been paid." She grabbed her purse from the seat.

Ian kept a grip on her elbow as he led her out of the door. The crowded street, bustling with activity, forbid them from holding a conversation, so she allowed him to lead her to his car.

He opened the passenger door and stepped aside while she slipped into the seat. As he got in himself, he slammed the door with enough force to shake the vehicle.

"Is something wrong, Ian?"

"Like what?"

"I don't know. You tell me."

His eyes, as cold as blue steel, raked over her appearance. "I didn't realize that you held your business meetings in a hotel."

"A restaurant that happens to be located in a hotel."

She smoothed the line of her linen skirt that had hiked up when she sat down. What was going through his mind? He couldn't possibly think her interest in sweet, old Mr. Merring was anything more than professional. Given his father's history with younger women, Ian might assume the worst of some wealthy businessman he'd never met. But he should have known her better.

"You spend a lot of time in the city," he noted.

"Because that's where my work is. Where would you think I would work from?"

"I have no idea."

"You have no idea what I do for a living, do you?"

"No." His answer came as no surprise but hurt all the same. She figured his grandfather would have mentioned something after their meeting, but apparently Ian hadn't cared enough to find out.

"You've known me two months now and you never even asked."

"I asked. You said you did freelance work. I assumed you did some kind of temp work in offices."

He'd remembered some offhanded comment she'd made while flaming mad and had decided that was all he needed to know.

"You never asked again, though. You didn't have enough interest in me or my life."

His jaw dropped open. "How can you say I have no interest in you?"

Shannon twisted her hands together in her lap. "I'm sorry. You are interested in having sex with me."

He groaned at her blunt description of their relationship. "It's more than that. I told you I just need some time."

"Well, while you're taking your sweet time, I still have a child to raise, and it's becoming clearer by the day that I'm going to be raising her alone." Her pain had receded, replaced by a rising anger. She took a deep breath and clenched her fingers into tight fists. "Drop me at the train station, please."

"Don't be ridiculous." He turned over the ignition and the engine roared to life.

For several moments they sat in silence, neither one glancing at the other. She locked her fingers together to control the trembling.

"Shannon?"

"What?" she asked, keeping her gaze on the windshield.

"What do you do for a living?"

"Now you want to know?" She laughed but she felt no humor. "Just drop me at Grand Central."

He hit the electronic locks and threw the car in gear. "I'll drive you."

As usual, Ian would do whatever he damn well pleased. She huddled into the corner of the bucket seat and braced herself for the long ride home. "Fine. Just don't talk to me."

The one-hour ride to Walton seemed to take an eternity. Ian's one attempt at striking a conversation with Shannon ended when she began singing a loud and off-key rendition of a song on the radio.

Okay. So he'd reacted badly. He hadn't thought himself capable of jealousy, an emotion he considered a waste of energy. But when he'd glanced across the restaurant, all he had seen was a well-dressed older man, who bore a resemblance to his own father, entertaining Shannon.

When he pulled into the driveway, he had to grab her wrist before she bolted. "Wait."

"Don't walk me in."

"I want to see Chelsea."

"Then you can take a walk next door. She's staying overnight with Wendy." Her declaration reminded him that if he hadn't been such a fool, they would be at his apartment right now making love instead of having an argument.

She pulled her hand free and quickly pushed her way out of the car.

He caught up to her on the porch. "Can we please talk now?"

"I've been trying to get you to talk since the beginning of our relationship but you kept putting me off." Her vacant stare cut like a knife. "Now, I need time, Ian. I think it would be best if we didn't see each other for a while."

Cupping his fingers over her shoulders, he eased her against a support beam. "All right. I behaved like a jerk. I apologize."

"This isn't about today. Your behavior was just a symptom of the problem. I will not live my life constantly defending myself. You aren't capable of trusting."

"I'll admit it doesn't come easy..."

Her eyes shimmered with unspent tears. "You are so sure that everyone is out for something that you don't stop to enjoy what you have. You're going to end up like your father, drifting in and out of meaningless relationships."

"Don't compare me to my father," he growled through tightly clenched teeth.

"Why? Because the women you chase aren't twenty-five? Give it a few years. Those will be the only women you can find who aren't looking for any commitment beyond a good time."

He stared at her bleakly, rocked by the sorrow he saw in her face. If he stayed, if she allowed him, he could soothe away the pain, make things right again. They both knew how she responded to him when he turned on the heat. He could transform her anger to arousal, her arousal to release. Afterward, she would despise him even more.

He rubbed his thumb across her tearstained cheek

and gave her a light kiss. His best hope was to respect her wishes and give her some time alone. Until he knew exactly what he was willing to give of himself, he had no right asking anything from her.

"Is it all right if I see Chelsea this weekend?"

The words seemed to be caught in her throat. She nodded and ducked under his arm. As he watched her disappear inside the house he felt as if he'd lost a part of himself.

For a long moment he stared at the door that had been shut in his face. He had to do something, but what? Walk inside and demand she listen to him? What could he say that wouldn't make the situation worse? He needed time to think. Hopefully, when he returned this weekend, she would be less emotional. All he had to do now was figure out how to explain himself. He didn't have one logical excuse for his behavior today.

Shannon flopped down into the oversize chair with a grunt. She hadn't gotten any sleep the night before and as soon as Chelsea left for preschool, Wendy was on her doorstep, full of unsolicited advice and neighborly cheer.

"Don't you think you're hitting the bottle a little hard?" Wendy ran a sweeping gaze over Shannon's less-than-attractive appearance.

She kicked off her fuzzy slippers and took another swig from her glass. "I'm entitled."

"Lay off the hard stuff. And mixing could be lethal." Wendy made a dive for the brownies while

Shannon cuddled her bottle of chocolate milk protectively against her chest. "Who told you this was going to help you get over a broken heart?"

"I think it was you."

"Not me. I said it relieves sexual frustration."

Shannon laughed bitterly. She had a hefty dose of that, as well. Of all the dumb things she'd done in her life, falling for Ian had been the crowning glory of her achievement in stupidity. She couldn't even blame him. He had been honest from the beginning. He wasn't looking for a permanent relationship.

Oddly, until Ian came into her life, she hadn't been looking for a relationship, either. She had viewed marriage as a battlefield—a war between two people that left innocent children as prisoners of war.

"Besides," Wendy cut in. "I'm no authority on heartbreak. I married my high school sweetheart."

"Great. I'm going to split my jeans and still feel like—"

"Watch your language." Wendy waved a scolding finger.

Shannon appreciated her friend's concerned interference, but she just wanted to be left alone to wallow in her misery. By the end of the day, she would have a bellyache to override her heartache. "Why don't you go home? I'm not going to kill myself over a man."

"I have to make sure you come down off this caffeine high." Wendy waved her hand at the spectacle before her. "What would Chelsea think if she saw you like this when she got back from school?"

"She would know I'm a hopeless hypocrite since I make her eat fruit while I horde the cookies."

Sympathy softened her friend's features. "Maybe when you see Ian this weekend he'll realize…"

"He won't." Suspicion and cynicism were too ingrained in his personality for him to trust her. If she allowed him, he would apologize his way back into her bed and then wait for their next misunderstanding to righteously rip her heart out again.

"If I leave, you're gonna sit here and feel sorry for yourself."

"If you stay, I'm going to gag you and then sit here and feel sorry for myself."

Wendy scrunched her nose at Shannon's threat.

"I'm really all right. Or I will be when I finish that plate of brownies."

With a shrug of defeat, Wendy settled back in her seat. "I hope you know it will take four hours on a treadmill to work off all that junk."

The doorbell rang. Shannon groaned. "Great! Why don't I throw a party?" She padded across the room to answer the door. Her stomach grumbled in protest from the rich chocolate.

"May I help you?" she asked the well-dressed man on her doorstep. Her own appearance by comparison was enough to frighten a troll.

"Are you Shannon Moore?"

"Yes."

He handed her an envelope without cracking a smile and turned on his heels to leave. As she unfolded the official-looking papers and began to read the document, the pain in her belly became acute. Her hands trembled.

"What is it?" Wendy asked, her voice wary.

"A message from Ian," Shannon snarled as she returned to the living room. "Seems he doesn't want to wait a year for his precious company so he's decided to sue me for control of Chelsea's inheritance."

What had been merely a heartache transformed into a blazing fury. The crushing weight of betrayal settled over her chest. She knew how slowly the court system worked. This wasn't an action he had decided upon yesterday out of spite. Why had he bothered to make love to her, make her fall in love with him if he had planned the lawsuit right from the start? Was he just using her for information? Her heart didn't want to accept that he could be that cold and calculating, but her head knew better. After all, he was his father's son.

She threw the document down on the table as if the very paper burned her skin.

"What are you going to do?" Wendy asked.

For a long moment she didn't answer. Shock. Undoubtedly she must be in shock for, suddenly, thankfully, she felt nothing. Just a numbing chill that obliterated all sensations from her body. Calmly, she raised her head. "I'm going to let him have control. As long as I have Chelsea, I don't give a damn what he does. We don't need him in our lives."

"That's just your hurt talking, Shannon. Maybe there's an explanation," Wendy offered feebly.

"I'm sure there is. Ian has a unique way of justifying everything. I just don't care to hear it." Shannon fell back into a chair and reached for her glass, raising a toast toward her friend. "Welcome to the nineties, where marriage is no longer required for relationships to end in bitter legal battles."

If he couldn't extend her the courtesy of telling her in person that he wanted control of Westervelt Properties, she would answer him in kind; through a lawyer. At least he hadn't attempted to gain custody of Chelsea. But then, she would have given him one hell of a fight if he'd tried.

Ian joined his grandfather in the living room. The rambling farmhouse usually afforded him a modicum of relaxation, but today nothing would ease his tension. After his meeting with Shannon on Monday, the week had gone progressively downhill. Work-related problems had kept him occupied during the days, but the nights had been too damn long.

Shannon would neither answer her phone nor return his messages. Although he'd spoken to Chelsea twice, the child was hardly a wealth of information. And he had stooped low enough to try to question his sister.

Adam stormed into the room. "What are you doing, Ian?"

Ian shook his head, surprised by the anger reflected in his grandfather's voice. "Visiting. I figured I'd catch you before you left for the office."

"I'm talking about Shannon."

Had she called Adam? She wasn't the type to involve others in her problems but unless his grandfather had ESP he couldn't know about their argument. "We had a little disagreement."

"A little one?" Adam bellowed. "I'd hate to see what you'd do if you had a really big fight."

"What are you talking about?"

"If you had wanted the financial statements you should have come to me yourself and I would have talked some sense into you. I didn't appreciate learning from a lawyer that you're suing my business partner's trustee. Especially Jenkins."

Ian felt as if he'd been sucker punched. He deserved the tongue-lashing and more. He had completely forgotten about the instructions he had given the lawyer at the reading of the will. No wonder Shannon had refused to come to the phone. "Wait a second—"

Adam waved a hand to cut Ian off. "What grounds were you planning to use? Incompetency? She could run this business better than you could right now."

"What do you mean?"

The older man let out a groan of disappointment. "Do you have any idea what she does for a living?"

That seemed to be the sixty-four-thousand-dollar question of the week. "It never came up."

"You mean, you never asked," Adam corrected as if he were scolding a child. "Lord, Ian, the woman understands the market better than most of our top agents. She's on the payroll of one of the largest securities firms in New York." He crossed his arms over his chest. "I won't be a party to this lawsuit."

"I'll call Jenkins and have him stop the suit before it's too late."

"It's already too late, boy. Shannon was served with the papers two days ago. What were you thinking?"

That was the problem. From the moment he'd met Shannon he hadn't been thinking at all. "I signed those papers before..."

"Before what?"

Before Shannon and Chelsea had become such an important part of his life. Before he had fallen in love with them. The realization stunned him.

"You'd better go talk to her."

Ian raked his hand through his hair. "She doesn't want to see me. She's made that clear."

"Maybe not, but you owe her the courtesy of explaining in person. Just imagine what she must have thought when she was served with the papers."

That he was vengeful? Cruel? And greedy, as well? He came to his feet. "You're right."

Adam raised an apologetic smile. "While you're already in a lousy mood, I have a box of your father's personal papers from the wall safe in the office. You might want to check through them before you toss them out."

The last thing Ian needed was another trip

through the emotional wringer. Or perhaps that was
just what he needed. He'd leaped to an awful lot of
wrong conclusions lately. He had to start facing
some facts.

Thirteen

Shannon coiled an elastic band through Chelsea's pigtail and straightened her collar. The child was usually cooperative on the mornings when she had Pee Wee Camp, but not today. She twisted and wiggled around as Shannon tried to dress her.

"Ian coming today?" Chelsea asked for the second time this morning and the hundredth time this week.

"No. Tomorrow." And not a moment sooner.

Shannon had already arranged for a high school girl to baby-sit so she wouldn't be around when Ian picked up his sister. Although she had no desire to even deal with him, she refused to make the child a pawn in their problems. Trying to keep her personal feelings for him hidden from Chelsea had proven a monumental task.

"Why he not come today?"

"He has to work." Shannon double knotted Chelsea's sneaker lace. "There. All finished. Let's get your snack and go wait for the bus."

With a smile, Shannon waved her niece off to camp, but her heart felt no joy. Just the same numbing, nagging emptiness that had blanketed her the past couple of days. Perhaps a jog around the neighborhood would give her a boost of energy.

She sprinted for a few blocks to raise her heart rate, then paced herself to make sure she had the stamina to get home. Her running shoes pounded the pavement. She didn't exercise as often as she used to, but as an alternative to sexual frustration, she might have to take it up again. Of course she wouldn't have this sexual frustration if Ian hadn't shown her how good sex could be.

Stop it! Stop thinking about him. She groaned aloud. Falling in love wasn't fatal. Many people survived the experience and went on to live healthy lives. But would she ever again feel that sense of wonder, anticipation—passion?

She picked up the pace, hoping to exhaust herself. A half hour later, when she returned to the house, she was winded and tired, but feeling stronger than she had in a while. At least until she saw the tall, broad-shouldered figure standing on the front landing. She was about to slip around to the back when he turned around.

Running her fingers through her hair, she tried to restore order to the damp strands. She approached without making eye contact.

"What are you doing here?" She opened the front door and stepped inside.

"You look whipped."

In a fit of pique, she slammed the door in his face. Of course she looked *whipped*. She hadn't been expecting him or she would have made damn sure she was a picture of poise and detached calm. Instead, she looked like a refugee.

Apparently undaunted by her greeting, Ian strolled into the house as if he had the right. "You really should learn to lock your doors."

Damn him! Why did he have to look so good? The horizontal lines of his rugby shirt emphasized his broad shoulders and powerful arms. Arms that only a week ago had cradled her while she slept. "I thought you weren't coming until tomorrow."

"I have a date with Chelsea tomorrow and I figured you'd make sure you weren't around. I need to speak with you."

"Why? Did you need more information for your lawsuit? My mother married money the second time around. My sister trapped a man with money. I must be after something, as well. Have you figured out what?"

"Cut me some slack here and listen for a second."

"Well, why stop with my gold-digging transgression? Maybe you can try to dig up enough on me to sue for custody of Chelsea, too? Oh, no. That would mean you'd have to make a commitment to someone other than yourself."

He winced at her angry snipe, but didn't rise to

the bait. Instead he folded his arms across his chest and calmly waited for her to finish her tirade. She hated the way he could rile her up while never losing control himself.

Since she couldn't remove him by means of force, she stepped aside and waved for him to enter the living room. "It's just as well. I have a few things to discuss myself." She scooped up a few dishes from the coffee table.

Ian's lips raised in a half grin. "Froot Loops for breakfast?"

After placing the bowls on the dining room table, she turned back to him. "Did you come here to discuss my dietary habits?"

His smile faded. "No."

"Then I'll go first." Shannon dropped down onto the corner of the sofa and folded her bare legs beneath her. She pulled the edges of the baggy T-shirt over her knees. "You're more than welcome to have control of Chelsea's shares of Westervelt Properties. I will, of course, send that in writing to your attorney and you can drop your lawsuit."

Ian lowered himself rigidly into the chair across from Shannon. He expected anger. He expected hurt. However, he hadn't prepared himself for the possibility that she would try to cut all ties with him. "Why?"

"Does it matter?"

"Yes."

Her hands trembled. She twisted her fingers together in her lap and inhaled a deep breath. "I was wrong to bribe you into a relationship with Chelsea.''

He arched an eyebrow. "Figuring that the only reason I'm here is to get the company?"

She met his challenging gaze with one of her own. "You're suing me, Ian. Is that an unreasonable conclusion to reach?"

Although he deserved it, her low opinion of him cut deep. "Well, you're too late. I put a stop to the suit and I don't want to buy her shares. I've decided to keep my little partner."

"Don't play games," she snapped. "Why don't you try being honest for a change?"

"Honest? Would you recognize the truth?"

She pushed a handful of hair back from her face, tucking the strands behind her delicate ears. Golden sparks of anger danced in her wide eyes. "Meaning?"

"Why didn't you tell me you were a successful financial consultant? If for no other reason, you could have enjoyed the pleasure of making me eat crow."

"I didn't think I should have to dangle my financial status over you to prove my worthiness. Besides, you never cared enough to ask."

"I didn't look down on you when I thought you were a clerical worker."

Raising her chin, she met his gaze. "But you didn't trust me, either. You still thought I was out for myself."

"No, I didn't," he denied firmly. Not in his heart, anyway. In truth, he was scared of what he felt for her so he'd tried to push her away. He might well have succeeded.

"Oh, come on." She came to her feet and paced the carpeted floor. "The thought was there. You pictured me stringing you along for all I could get out of you. Well, I've had my share of offers if that's what I wanted. Your father included."

A cold chill washed over him. "What?"

"Wesley wanted to get together with me, to discuss 'financial arrangements' regarding Chelsea. He hinted that there might be something in it for me if we came to an understanding. I sent him a letter terminating the child support agreement he'd had with my sister. Apparently, he wasn't too broken up over the fact. I never heard from him again."

The thought of his father propositioning Shannon brought a new wave of anger, but not toward her. He had seen her letter only yesterday, in his father's personal papers, but hadn't realized what precipitated the correspondence.

"I'm sorry," was all he could think of to say.

"There's no need to be. I never held your father's sins against you."

Unlike him, she might as well have added. He had allowed her sister's affair with his father to cloud his judgment concerning Shannon. "Does it make any difference if I tell you I began that lawsuit before I met you or Chelsea?"

"Yeah, it lets me know you're not a total bastard. But it doesn't change anything. If you came here to see how I was doing, I'm fine. I got hurt but that's my fault. You gave me no reason to assume you wanted the same things I did.''

"What do you want?"

"Security. Not financial, but emotional. A stable family life for Chelsea and myself.'' Her soft laugh was tinged with irony. "That *is* your fault. Before I met you, I avoided the notion of family life. I let my delusional fantasies blur my view of reality, but I've got my feet back on the ground now.'' She walked into the kitchen and poured herself a large glass of chocolate milk.

Ian followed. He wouldn't allow her to escape before he had his say. "On one thing, we agree. Chelsea needs stability. I never felt that as a child and subsequently, my views on relationships are somewhat skewed.''

"Are you suggesting I can't give that to her?'' Shannon's voice rang with defensive anger.

"She's three years old. Still young enough to forget the start she had in life. But she needs a normal family life, not the guardianship of her aunt, however loving, and sporadic visits from her brother.''

Her jaw clenched. "I don't like where this is going.''

"Where do you think I'm heading.''

"You're suggesting adoption?''

"Yes.''

Her glare could freeze a molten volcano. "Forget it. I'm doing fine with her. She's a happy child.''

"I know.''

"Then why put her up for adoption? I obviously don't find her the inconvenience you do.'' She pressed her hands against the counter to still the trembling.

Did she really believe he would make a suggestion so callous? He loved Chelsea. Enough to forgive his father for the past. Whether Wesley intended it or not, he had left Ian something far more precious than money in the will. His father had given him a chance for the loving family life he had never known as a child.

"I meant *we* should adopt her."

"Us?" She stopped in her tracks and whirled toward him. "And then what? Shuffle her around between us like divorced parents with joint custody? You think that's stability? Let me tell you from experience, it doesn't work."

Her features clouded in unmistakable sadness. He reached for her, but she ducked under his outstretched hand.

"That wasn't how I pictured it."

She tossed her hands up in the air. "Well, what were you thinking, Ian?"

He shoved his hands into his pockets and muttered, "I figured we'd get married first."

His declaration stunned her into immobility. "You figured *what?*"

Ian noted the look of panic on her face and wondered if he'd made a big mistake. He had stayed up half the night searching for just the right words to tell her how he felt. Instead, his untimely proposal came out sounding as if he had offered for Chelsea's sake.

"That didn't exactly come out right."

"Apparently. Mr. Nothing Heavy or Serious is talking about marriage? Did somebody hit you over the head with a lead pipe?"

"In a way." He certainly felt as if he'd been clobbered. That his beautiful assailant had ambushed him without raising a single hand didn't lessen the impact. The thought of losing her was far more frightening than a walk down the aisle.

"And precisely how long do you think it would be before you began to feel trapped?"

He slipped a hand around her back and pulled her closer. After an initial struggle, she grudgingly gave up, but her body remained tense. "I'm already trapped, Shannon. Trapped in a world of dinner for one in a silent apartment. Damn it, I can't even sleep because you're not there."

"If memory serves me, you once said you couldn't sleep *with* me," she reminded him with a bitter laugh.

His mother had always warned him to mince his words carefully to make it easier when he had to eat them. Now he understood what she had meant. He smiled sheepishly. "That's because I knew this would happen if I did."

"What would happen?"

"I would like the feeling of you curled up next to me." He massaged the warm skin below her shoulder blades. Despite her tension, she reacted to his touch. "Like the way you wake me up to make love in the middle of the night."

Her cheeks flushed and she chewed her bottom lip. "It's not as if you were fighting me off."

A chuckle escaped through his pursed lips.

She glared.

"I'm not an idiot, even if I behaved like one," he said by way of explanation. In the long silence that followed, Ian held his breath.

She tipped her head to one side and peered at him from beneath her dark lashes. "It won't work."

"Why?"

"Something's missing from your little scenario."

"What?"

"Love."

One simple word that had always scared the hell out of him.

"Are you saying you've fallen out of love with me? Is that why you're sitting around in my T-shirt drowning your sorrows in a bottle of chocolate milk?"

She exhaled a slow groan. "I was talking about you."

"I love you." There, he said the words and it wasn't nearly as difficult as he'd imagined. Perhaps because for once in his life, he truly felt loved in return. The hard part would be convincing Shannon, who had every reason to doubt him.

"You expect me to believe you now?"

"What do I have to gain by lying?" he asked pointedly.

"What do you gain by telling the truth?" she countered, the doubt ringing in her voice.

"A life," he said simply. "Because without you and Chelsea, I don't have one."

The tension began to ease from her body. Her

adamant fury seemed to be fading to wary confusion. "Don't you think marriage is a bit extreme?"

He frowned. "Isn't that what you wanted?"

"No. I wanted some kind of commitment from you, not a piece of paper you felt forced to sign." Her soft words were choked with emotion.

"No one is forcing me. I want to spend the rest of our lives together. I love you, Shannon. I need you in my life."

Shannon froze. Could she really believe him? She wanted to but she wasn't anxious to have her heart broken yet another time. "I can't go through this again."

"Trust me, just once more. I promise you won't regret it." His voice shook with raw emotion.

"You better mean that, Ian, or I might just have to kill you."

He brushed at a tear streaming down her cheek and left his hand to rest on the side of her face. "If you send me out of your life, you will kill me."

His honest admission melted the last of her reservations. She draped her arms around his neck. Relief mingled with jubilation. "I wouldn't want that on my conscience."

He slipped his hand under the cotton T-shirt and stroked the skin along her stomach. Her pulse quickened. She squeezed her eyes shut and tried to fight off the erotic sensations his touch engendered. The speed with which he could arouse her never failed to amaze her.

"So, you'll marry me, right?" he asked.

Trust Ian to use her aroused state to his advantage. She hesitated just long enough to make him sweat. Until now, she had given up any hope that he might come around.

His fingers dipped lower and teased the elastic of her running shorts. She let out a moan. "All right. I'll marry you."

The seductive onslaught came to an abrupt and frustrating halt. "When?"

She almost laughed at the desperate tone to his voice. Once he made up his mind, he didn't waste any time getting what he wanted. "You're going to be married the rest of your life. Don't you want to enjoy the last of your freedom?"

Arching an eyebrow, he asked, "Are you suggesting that I go out and have one last fling?"

No. She didn't like the sound of that at all and he knew it, too. She leaned closer and bit his shoulder.

"Ouch. What was that for?"

"Marking my territory."

"Not necessary." Ian leaned against the counter looking more relaxed and peaceful than she had ever seen him. For a man who had fought marriage and commitment with such fierce passion, he looked mighty pleased with today's outcome. "You're going to have me all to yourself."

She inched closer and fitted herself between his solid legs. "You think so? I have to share you with Chelsea and that is one child who is very possessive about her toys. And you are her favorite toy." Mine, too, Shannon thought, and she was definitely in the mood to play with him today.

"Well, then, after the adoption, we'll have to give her a little brother or sister to fuss over."

"Is that another of your brilliant ideas like the kitten to teach her responsibility?"

He shook his head. "No. This is one decision you have to have a major say in."

"Then, I say yes." Her heart, which this morning had been broken, now swelled with love. She reached for the snap on his jeans and yanked open the fly. "Why wait for the adoption? Let's start now."

*   *   *   *   *

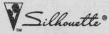

BEVERLY BARTON

Continues the twelve-book series— 36 Hours—in April 1998 with Book Ten

NINE MONTHS

Paige Summers couldn't have been more shocked when she learned that the man with whom she had spent one passionate, stormy night was none other than her arrogant new boss! And just because he was the father of her unborn baby didn't give him the right to claim her as his wife. Especially when he wasn't offering the one thing she wanted: his heart.

For Jared and Paige and *all* the residents of Grand Springs, Colorado, the storm-induced blackout was just the beginning of 36 Hours that changed *everything!* You won't want to miss a single book.

Available at your favorite retail outlet.

SC36HRS10

DIANA PALMER
ANN MAJOR
SUSAN MALLERY

RETURN TO WHITEHORN

In **April 1998** get ready to catch the bouquet. Join in the excitement as these bestselling authors lead us down the aisle with three heartwarming tales of love and matrimony in Big Sky country.

A very engaged lady is having second thoughts about her intended; a pregnant librarian is wooed by the town bad boy; a cowgirl meets up with her first love. Which Maverick will be the next one to get hitched?

Available in **April 1998**.

Silhouette's beloved **MONTANA MAVERICKS** returns in Special Edition and Harlequin Historicals starting in February 1998, with brand-new stories from your favorite authors.

Round up these great new stories at your favorite retail outlet.

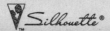